Praise for Grégoire Delacourt

'A gorgeous little novel . . . a fable-like tale of how money can't buy happiness'

Stylist on *The List of My Desires*

'An affecting story of a couple thrown into turmoil by their dreams and longings. A beautiful tale'

Psychologies on *The List of My Desires*

'A runaway bestseller that looks set to follow the success of *The Elegance of the Hedgehog*. But that's not surprising – Grégoire Delacourt is an author who knows how to make his readers feel happy . . . [he] describes the dilemmas of the heart and the vagaries of fate with tenderness and empathy'

Elle on *The List of My Desires*

'A massive seller across Europe, this little book of Gallic charm is likely to warm British hearts too'

Choice on *The List of My Desires*

'A sweet and poignant novella . . . Beautifully written, readers will devour it in one sitting, turning the final page with one adage in their heads: the other man's grass is not always greener'

Irish Examiner on *The List of My Desires*

Grégoire Delacourt is the bestselling author of five novels and has won several literary awards. *The List of My Desires* was a runaway number-one bestseller in France, with rights sold in thirty-three countries, and was selected for the Waterstones Book Club in the UK. *We Only Saw Happiness*, published in France as *On ne voyait que le bonheur*, was longlisted for the Prix Goncourt 2014. Grégoire lives in Paris, where he runs an advertising agency with his wife.

www.gregoire-delacourt.com

Also available from W&N

The List of My Desires
The First Thing You See

we only

saw

happiness

Grégoire Delacourt

Translated from the French by
by Anthea Bell

WEIDENFELD & NICOLSON

A W&N PAPERBACK

First published in Great Britain in 2016 by Weidenfeld & Nicolson
This paperback edition published in 2017 by Weidenfeld & Nicolson
an imprint of the Orion Publishing Group Ltd
Carmelite House, 50 Victoria Embankment
London EC4Y 0DZ
An Hachette UK Company

1 3 5 7 9 10 8 6 4 2

First published in France in 2014
as *On ne voyait que le bonheur*
by Editions Jean-Claude Lattès

A CIP catalogue record for this book is
available from the British Library.

ISBN (mass market paperback) 978 1 4746 0099 6
ISBN (eBook) 978 1 4746 0005 7

Printed in Great Britain by Clays Ltd, St Ives plc

www.orionbooks.co.uk

This one is for the girl who was seated on the car.
She made me fly all the way to Dumbo.

'Don't shake me; I am full of tears.'

Henri Calet, *Peau d'ours*

A life, and I was well placed to know it, is worth between thirty and forty thousand euros.

A life. The cervix finally dilated to ten centimetres, breath coming short, birth, blood, tears, joy, pain; the first bath, first teeth, first steps; new words, falling off a bike, braces from the dentist, the fear of tetanus; jokes, cousins, holidays, allergies to cat hair; tantrums, sweets, cavities; lies, sidelong glances, laughter, wonder, scarlet fever, gangly bodies shooting out in every direction, too-big ears, breaking voices, erections, mates, girls, blackhead remover, betrayals, doing good, wanting to change the world and kill the bastards, all the bastards; hangovers, shaving foam; heartache, love, wanting to die, the Baccalauréat, university, romantic novels, the Stones, rock 'n' roll, drugs, curiosity, the first job, first pay packet, painting the town red to celebrate it, getting engaged, getting married, cheating for the first time, loving again, the need for love, the sweetness it brings, nostalgia, the sudden speeding up of time, a shadow on the right lung, difficulty urinating in the morning, new embraces, skin, the texture of that skin, a suspect mole, tremors, savings, the warmth we seek, planning for afterwards, when they're grown up, when there's just the two of us again, travel, blue oceans, Blood and Sand cocktails in the bar of a hotel with an unpronounceable name in Mexico or some such place; a smile, clean sheets, the smell of freshness, together again, a prick as hard as stone, a headstone; a life.

It's worth between thirty and forty thousand euros if you get run over.

Twenty or twenty-five thousand if you're a child.

A little more than a hundred thousand if you're in a plane that crashes down from the sky, taking you and two hundred and twenty-seven other lives with it.

How much were ours worth?

Part One

Fifty Thousand Dollars

Les Dossiers de l'écran, the weekly television programme, featured the Lindbergh case, so we'd been talking about it at school. I was nine years old. We'd been told all about the kidnapping of the twenty-month-old baby — curly-haired, chubby — and the ransom demand: fifty thousand dollars, a fortune in 1932. And then the terrible thing had happened. The money had been paid and the body of Charles Augustus Lindbergh was recovered, in an advanced state of decomposition, with a major fracture to the skull. The man responsible was caught and put to death in the electric chair. We felt scared leaving school that day. Many of us ran home; I walked quickly, looking over my shoulder, and arrived at my house pale, trembling and wet. My sisters made fun of me: he fell into the water, he fell into the water, what a stupid boy. They were barely five. My mother, guessing I was distraught, stubbed out her menthol cigarette – slowly, almost savouring the action. I threw myself into her arms, and she recoiled slightly, perhaps in surprise. We were not a family for affectionate words or hugs. We kept our emotions in place, under wraps. If someone kidnapped me, I asked my mother, shivering, would you and Papa give them your money? Would you save me? Her eyes, two incredulous marbles, lit up and widened, and then she smiled at me. Her smiles were infrequent, and all the more beautiful for that. She swept back a lock of my hair. My forehead was cold, my lips almost blue.

Of course, Antoine, she murmured. We'd give our lives for you. Our whole lives.

My heart stopped racing.

I never was kidnapped. So they never had to give their lives for me. But I was not saved.

Eighty Euros

I tell you, it was to die for. I found her on the internet. I was scared stiff at first, paranoid. Thinking someone might try to film me or blackmail me. Or I'd get my face smashed in, my money stolen or my watch, my teeth knocked out. Scared shitless. I'm nearly forty, like you, Antoine, and I can stand up for myself, know what I mean? But this was different. When I got there I was really bricking it. There was a keypad and a seedy little entrance hall. The smell of cooking, at eleven in the morning, a damp staircase, like you get in those cheesy movies. It was on the fourth floor. My heart was thumping. I felt my thirty-eight years catching up with me as I climbed the stairs. I need to get some exercise, I thought, at least ride a bike. I've heard that's good for your plumbing. My heart felt like it was about to explode. Can you imagine the look on Fabienne's face, if she was confronted by my corpse. What the hell

7

was he doing there? What did my husband think he was doing at eleven in the morning, on the fourth floor of an apartment block, with a *tart* for heaven's sake? I slowed down a bit. Stopped to catch my breath on the third-floor landing. Like an old mutt taking a rest between two throws of a tennis ball that has been chucked a long, long way, just to piss the dog off. I don't like dogs. They smell bad when it rains. And then a dog gets old really quickly, it gets cancer or something and then you have to put it down. On the fourth floor I see four doors, I don't know which one it is. But one of them is open, or rather, it's opening. I move quietly, cautiously, still scared shitless. I might not even be able to get a hard-on, I think to myself. She's on the other side of that door. Bloody hell, she's small, she doesn't look a thing like her photo. But she has a nice smile. It isn't even a studio flat, just a room. It's almost dark, and all I can make out is a bed, a computer, and a box of tissues. I give her the eighty euros, she counts them, and hey presto, they disappear. Then she comes over and opens my fly, getting straight to the point. I look around me. Nothing. No red camera light. Just a miserable, damp room. In fact, it's lucky that Fabienne doesn't like doing that sort of thing. (Silence.) Because I don't much like asking her, it sounds really crude if you have to ask. *Give me a blow job.* That isn't the language of love. Nor is

8

fellatio. Even if you use something funny, like *suck me off*, it's still not a very romantic thing to say. I love my wife, I don't want to talk dirty to her. But that's what the little tart is for, for all those words jammed inside me. To deal with my kind of cowardice. We men can't win, you know. So I get sucked off for eighty euros, and I don't upset Fabienne.

FFF swallowed the last of his beer, heaved a tiny sigh of pleasure, put his glass down delicately and then looked at me. He raised his eyebrows, smiled with his eyes and got to his feet.

No, that's OK, it's on me, I said when FFF put his hand in his pocket.

Thanks, Antoine. See you tomorrow.

And I was left alone.

I lit another cigarette and inhaled deeply. The smoke burned my mouth, my chest; I felt pleasantly dizzy. The waitress came over and cleared away our empty glasses. I ordered another beer. I didn't want to go back to my empty life. She had a beautiful face, a beautiful mouth, a pretty body. Only half my age too. But I didn't dare.

Five Francs

My parents had wanted a child in order to become a family quickly – that is, a couple who wouldn't be asked questions. A child would put a certain distance between them and the rest of the world. Even back then.

When she arrived home from the maternity hospital, my mother went straight back to her room, where she would shut herself in to smoke menthols and read Françoise Sagan. She got her figure back quickly, like that of the writer; the grace of a twenty-year-old. And when she sometimes went out to buy vegetables, powdered milk or a packet of cigarettes and she was asked how the baby was doing, she'd reply: Oh, he's fine, I think, he's fine, and people were bowled over by her smile.

I made the trip home from hospital in their little 2CV. My father drove carefully, aware, I suppose, of the fragility of what he was transporting: more than three kilos of flesh and internal organs, seventy-five centi-litres of blood and, most importantly, an open, pulsating fontanelle that one clumsy gesture could easily have destroyed. He dropped us off outside the building with-out getting out of the car. His arms did not shield me from any random violence that might have occurred between the car and the white cot in the bedroom. Instead, he left my mother to settle me in on her own, to marvel at the most beautiful baby in the world on her own, to try, on her own, to see in my nose the nose of one of my grandmothers, in my mouth the mouth of some other relative. He left us alone, he didn't take his wife in his arms, he didn't dance a jig. He simply went back to the pharmacy where he had been working for over a year, under the proprietor, a Monsieur Lapchin, a widower with no heirs who was very happy to have recruited my father. Apparently, my father could work miracles. He made up creams that worked on spotty adolescents, with a 4 per cent benzoyl peroxide base; he provided panic-stricken ladies with poison for rats, mice, spiders, cockroaches and sometimes a little some-thing to cure the blues: three drops on your tongue before you go to bed and in the morning you'll feel right as rain. That'll be five francs, Madame Jeanmart. Oh, how convenient, I just happen to have a brand-new note, here you go. Five francs isn't much to pay for a little happiness, thank you; no, thank you. My father had studied chemistry, he loved poetry, but his dreams of winning the Nobel Prize had vanished the day my mother crossed his path. She *demagnetised* me, he would later say, coldly, uttering the word as he might have said *solubility*. Or *polymerization*. She made him lose his bearings, his head, his trousers – which accounts for me – and a few hairs. They had met on 4 July at the Place Aristide-Briand in Cambrai. She was with her sisters. He was with his brothers. Their eyes met, then lingered. She was tall, slender, a Venetian blonde with dark eyes; he was tall, slender, with brown hair and eyes as green as water. They were spellbound, even if, back then, you behaved with decorum when under a spell: nothing more than a smile, a promise to meet again, a handshake. They did meet again, the very next day at the Montois bakery. My mother would later tell me that in daylight, without the fireworks, without a glass of champagne in her hand or the sweet sense of euphoria, she hadn't found my father quite so spellbinding. But there it was, he had green eyes, and she had always dreamed of meeting a man with green eyes; even if no one ever dreamed of meeting a laboratory assistant. They had made promises to each other; they had introduced one another to their parents. The young man was studying chemistry. The young woman was not studying anything. He was twenty, she was seventeen. They got married six months later. On 14 January. The wedding photos, thank goodness, were in black and white. So you couldn't see their blue lips, or my mother's extreme pallor, her little Venetian blonde hairs standing up like prickles. It was cold. And already you could sense the chill that had numbed their love and darkened those green eyes.

For as long as I can remember; for as long as I have searched for answers, for as long as I have wept, it seems that my parents never did love each other.

Twenty-Seven Euros

I didn't have time to finish my beer. My phone vibrated and a number came up; my father's wife's number.

I heard her voice, a voice that could soar, could sing Rachmaninov's *Vocalise*, Schubert's *Ave Maria*, with the church choir.

Her voice, suddenly; devastated.

We've just left the doctor's it's terrible just terrible I don't know what to say what to tell you but it's your father it's about your father they don't really know yet but it's not good news there are things there are traces it's his colon that's where it started and I asked the doctor if they were certain it was that if it was the disease with the name you can't say out loud and he looked at me he looked so sad he's a good GP he knows your father well he's been your father's GP for ages and he was so sad that I realised I'm not an idiot you know I'm not your mama but I do love your papa I take great care of him I take care of what he eats he stopped smoking you know he stopped for me long ago because I couldn't take it any more I was so worried but it isn't his lungs it's his colon that's where it started the doctor said but it's even worse think of that as if there could be anything worse than really bad it's his liver it's spread to his liver stage four he said in his sad way I don't know what to do when it's the liver it's all over I know that everyone knows that and everyone knows it spreads too I wanted to cry and tear my hair out and stab myself I was just waiting to finally retire so I could enjoy being with him and now well now it's over it's as if life is all over and useless it's not fair it's horrible we were going to Le Touquet next month I'd rented a ground-floor apartment so it wouldn't be too tiring for him call me back if you like if you can it's horrible and at the end of all that he asked me for twenty-seven euros just think twenty-seven euros to be told the man I love is going to die.

Twenty-seven euros.

I paid for the beers. Looked around me. The terrace was full now; people were laughing, people were smoking, people were alive. Nothing threatened them. I rose with difficulty; suddenly I was carrying the weight of my father. I was carrying the weight of the silence between us; I was carrying our moments of cowardice, every last one; those tiny mistakes that, millimetre by millimetre, on the scale of a lifetime, had taken us down the wrong path. To a dead end. A purple wall. The waitress smiled at me, and I wanted to cry, to throw myself into her arms, into her pale tenderness, I wanted to dare say the words that plunge you into mourning and set you free, my father is dying and I'm going to be an orphan I'm frightened I don't want to be alone I don't want to fall, and I wanted to hear her say I'm here, Monsieur, I'm here, I'll stay with you, don't be frightened, don't be frightened any more, there, lay your head there, against my breasts, don't think about a single thing.

But I didn't dare.

I never dared.

Two Francs Twenty

I don't know if I loved my father.

I liked his hands, they never shook. I liked his recipe for lemonade made with bicarbonate of soda. I liked the smell of his experiments. The noises he'd make when they didn't work. The noises he'd make when they did. I liked the way he unfolded his newspaper in the morning, in the blue kitchen of our big house. His eyes when he read the obituaries. His voice when he told my mother: this man was the same age as me, can you imagine? He was proud to still be alive. My mother would roll her eyes disdainfully; she was beautiful in her small, elegant contempt. I liked waiting for him in the evenings after school, outside the pharmacy. Through the window, I would watch him explaining things with extravagant gestures. I watched the ladies who were in love with him. The temptations. My father wasn't handsome, but women liked him. His white coat made him look like a scientist. His youth beguiled them. And his green eyes. Ah, those green eyes. Behind the scenes, Monsieur Lapchin gloated. Business was booming. Customers came to the pharmacy for all sorts of things, for anything. For ethylene, ethanol, strong glue. They came a long way. From Raismes, from Jenlain, from Saint-Aubert. The ladies came to see my father, Monsieur André. They didn't want to be served by anyone else, they arrived looking their best, they stood in line. They expected magic potions, beauty creams, slimming ointments. They liked to imagine his fingers on their skin, those hands that never shook and mixed marvellous concoctions. They all wanted him to choose them, but she was the one he chose: the woman with a wine stain on her silk blouse, a stain that looked like blood, like a broken heart. Come back tomorrow, Mademoiselle. And the next day there was a potion containing ammonia and her blouse was as good as new. She had two firm breasts under that blouse, a look, a smile. And my father asked her out to the Montois bakery. They've been together for nearly thirty years now.

Over the past thirty years he's been known to smile. He never did when our family was still together.

I was about to turn six. My mother had just given birth to my two sisters, identical twins; they may as well have been Siamese twins. Anne and Anna. Anna was the younger, arriving seven minutes and eighteen seconds after her sister. A breech birth. An episiotomy. A bloodbath. At the time my father had a beige Citroen GS with synthetic leather seats in a drab dark brown. He brought my mother and my sisters back from the maternity hospital in that car. He parked outside our house and went up to the pink room. He and my mother put the girls in their rose-pink lace-trimmed cots, he looked at them for a long time, marvelling, he even shed tears; then he took my mother in his arms and danced with her. He whispered thank you, thank you, they're wonderful, they're so beautiful, they're so like you; and my mother, also whispering, said, you don't know me, André, don't talk nonsense. When he went downstairs again he found me in the sitting room. He jumped. Oh, there you are. You can go up and see your sisters if you like. I didn't move. I just wanted to be in his arms. I just wanted to know that he still loved me, that I still existed, that I had a name and a father.

Here.

It was the first and only time I saw his hands shake.

Here, there's two francs twenty, go and buy me a packet of Gitanes. I need you now.

You see, I don't know if I loved my father.

When exactly does a man realise that he will never be a hero?

Four Francs Fifty

I walked away from the terrace, leaving behind the laughter, people meeting each other for the first time, FFF's eighty-euro piece of heaven, and plunged into the terrifying shadows of the night.

From which wild beasts have been known to emerge.

He's in the bedroom he's resting, she told me when I arrived at their place. He's in denial he keeps talking about the *incident* it's kind of you to come by but I don't think we should disturb him I'll tell him you came he'll be pleased about that he's going to need support and you know how proud he is so it's not going to be easy he always thinks he's stronger and more robust than everyone else I'm so sad if only you knew how sad I am it's kind of you to come by oh darn it I didn't want to cry but now I can't help it oh I'm glad he isn't seeing me like this a woman crying isn't a pretty sight it's frightening it looks so ugly when your make-up runs oh what's happening to us is so horrendous.

I put my arms round her and let her cry for a long time. I thought of the tears my mother used to shed, when she was alone, mourning the life she did not have. Green eyes aren't everything, she told me one day, they're not intoxicating, they find you in the night, they can even be frightening.

After the arrival of my twin sisters, my mother began to sleep in a separate room. Abstinence is better than a lack of passion, she said. Later, she would take several lovers and lose herself in fantasies. She would drink pale ale, and she never gave up her menthols, even though people disapproved; and in the haze of smoke she would dream of the lives she might have led, by the seaside where the wind blows off hats and reddens cheeks; those perfect places where you can shout the words that hurt because the wind muffles them and no one can hear. *Sadness*, *grief*, *sorrow*, *cowardice*.

My mother didn't like herself enough to be happy.

One night she had come and lain down beside me on my little bed. I moved up, pressing myself close to the wall, so happy that she was there. She didn't say anything for some time. I listened to the soothing sound of her breath, finding once more one of those moments of peace – rare as they were – that intense joy that I experienced whenever she let me stay with her in the sitting room, while she read and smoked. I loved the sour smell of the little fog that surrounded her, I wanted to drink it in, to impregnate myself with it. Menthol, that was my mother's smell; I wanted it to cling to me because I missed her caresses, her words, her gaze. Later, after she left, I would ask my father to concoct the scent for me, which he did, based on a $C_{10}H_{20}O$ formula enriched with essential oil of peppermint. She lay there beside me for a long time, and then, just when I thought she had fallen asleep, the words came out, both sweet and serious: Never be like your father, Antoine, be brutal, be strong, help yourself, shake women up, turn their heads, make them dream, make promises even if you can't keep them, we all live on hope not reality. Reality is for donkeys and idiots, dinner at 7.30 each evening, putting out the bins, a goodnight kiss, little pastries for four francs fifty on Sundays at the Montois bakery, life goes wrong so quickly, Antoine, so quickly.

Her tears fell on my neck, they burned me while I pretended to sleep.

My father's wife now dried her tears and thanked me again for coming, thanked me for my kindness. But it wasn't kindness, it was cowardice. I'm afraid of harm, of pain, of decrepitude; I'm still afraid of being abandoned, of being cold and hungry; I'm afraid of a life without grace or love. I haven't turned into the man my mother dreamed I would become, I didn't have the courage for that.

I kissed my father's wife, and then I went home.

Thirty Thousand Euros

The ball had gone over the garden wall. The little boy had run out to retrieve it. He had crossed the road without looking and the motorbike was unable to avoid him. The skid marks showed that it was not going much over the speed limit. The child had been knocked down, hitting his head hard on the tarmac. He had spent six days in a coma. The biker had skidded about thirty metres with his left leg stuck under the 180 kilos of his bike. He had to have his foot amputated.

I was sent to check the large Honda Hornet involved in the accident.

That's what I do for a living. I have to see what isn't seen, explain what can't be explained. For both insurance companies. There were many things to be taken into account in this accident: compensation for the distress suffered, for personal injury (the permanent loss of one foot), damage to quality of life (the foot again), loss of income, healthcare and rehabilitation costs, reimbursement for or repair of the vehicle, etc. The exhausts, the sprockets and the cylinder head of the motorbike had been modified so it was considered to be out of control from a legal standpoint: which could mean a fine of thirty thousand euros, two years in prison.

So the biker would get no compensation. The child's parents were going to bring charges against him. He would lose and would have to pay damages to the little footballer out of his own pocket. Basically, he was screwed.

On several occasions I've felt intoxicated by the idea of being able to change other people's lives. At best I've been an angel, at worst a total monster, above suspicion; I could keep quiet about the state of the motorbike, for instance, and let my client off the hook – minus a foot, yes, but almost a hundred thousand euros better off.

Enough to start a new life, to soak up the sun, drink Blood and Sand cocktails at the bar of a hotel with an unpronounceable name in Mexico or some such place. To live out what we all dream of doing and never really do. My mother would have liked a hundred thousand euros too, she would have liked to tell the chemist that there was no chemistry between them, and then leave; she would have liked to have been abducted, eaten by a cannibal, devoured by passion, been burnt out by excess.

But I didn't dare. I never dared. I am paid to pay out as little as possible. I am paid to have no heart and no compassion. I have no right to offer a hand to a ship-wrecked sailor, there is no place in me for pity or affection, for any kind of humanity; these words are unknown. My client was maimed and his life would be screwed. Which mine was, too, right from the very start.

Where does cowardice begin, Léon? In the eyes of your mother, which she couldn't tear away from the two green eyes that met hers one 14 July, on the Place Aristide-Briant? In the sighs of a chemistry student who gave up the idea of changing the world for a girl who loved the colour of his eyes? In menthol-scented smoke that gently anaesthetised you, making you renounce, day after day, the beauties of this world? In the hands that abandon a child to his own devices?

Where does it begin? It doesn't take a suicidal mother, an absentee father, an adult who hits you or lies to you. It doesn't take tragedy or bloodshed. One nasty remark as you come out of school is enough; you know something about that. A maternal kiss that fails to soar into the air is enough, smiles that do not alight on your shoulders like a feather. Someone who doesn't love you is enough.

I knew, from very early on, that I was a coward.

Fifty Centimes

As a child I did try to be strong.

I signed up to learn judo, but during my third class a green belt not much older than me humiliated me with the cross arm lock known as *juji gatame*. Having discovered that words, if well placed, could hit as hard as fists – my mother had delivered a blow to my father's solar plexus with You're such a disappointment to me, André – I turned to drama.

I learned to breathe. To project my voice. It would be better to say *shut up* in a deep voice rather than a nasal one, and much more threatening to have a taut body than a shrivelled one. I learned that you have to make an impression, and I wasn't impressive, I didn't have the weight or solidity of the kind of man my mother dreamed of. My parents had not swooned over me at the maternity hospital, and they did not do so later – I dare say there was no reason to. All the same,

I've known several women. I've been seduced. Some have said they would die for me, some have wanted to live with me. They have wanted children or affection. They've dreamt about me, they've expected things of me, they've wanted to drink cocktails with me in Mexico or some such place. They have wanted me to be happy.

But before such delights occurred, I was cast as one of two removal men in Feydeau's *La main passe*, our end-of-year school play. It wasn't a speaking role. I felt ashamed, I felt hurt, and if I was to fall from grace, I must not fall alone. I still wanted to be strong. I had noticed a boy called Frédéric Froment in the play-ground. A little runt with aluminium-framed glasses, milk-bottle lenses, the kind you'd be happy to lose in a supermarket or on the beach. I suggested he might be my friend. He had looked me up and down then smiled, genuinely touched, and I was cross with myself. Already. I asked him round for tea after school, and he accepted with a pleasure that still astonishes me to this day. We were going through the Monstrelet garden when my cowardice swept it all away.

Fight.

What?

Come on, if you're a man, fight.

I was already clenching my fists, ready to strike.

Fight. Defend yourself. I came closer. Threatening. Coward, such a coward.

Come on then, come on, fight.

His arms were still dangling by his sides. One of mine shot forwards like an arrow to punch him in the mouth; my skin broke on contact with his teeth. I bled, he bled.

I thought you wanted to be friends with me.

Then my cowardice burst into tears. Frédéric Froment drew closer and from his bleeding mouth came the words that condemned me: I know what it's like not being strong, I don't blame you. I'd have hit me too. I'd have hit me.

My bloodied hand shook his. We didn't yet know it, but we were going to be friends, and we ought to have been friends for ever.

At the bakery on Rue Crèvecœur I bought him a Mars bar for fifty centimes, a pathetic apology. He looked at me with sad little eyes like a beaten dog. That'f nife of you, but I fink you'f broken one of my teef.

That was the day that FFF was born, Léon.

Frigging Frédéric Froment.

Six Francs

My mother loved to read. She used to read Sagan, Cardinale, Barjavel. As soon as she got up she sat down to read, and a local Polish woman looked after me. After that I went to nursery and in the evenings my mother would pay babysitters six francs an hour, even though she was right there, in the sitting room. She didn't move from her spot and her eyes shone. My father claimed it was because she was sad, but I knew it was because of the beer that she drank, sometimes all day long. One day she told me she was too young to have a child. It's not that I didn't want you, she said, I didn't want me. I did not understand. She tried to explain: she'd never dreamed of being a good little wife and mother. It didn't interest her, that was all. But what about me? I asked. You love me, Mama? Do you love me? The same question that you are asking, Léon. She replied: Of course. Of course, but what use is that?

I grew up surrounded by scents that weren't hers, in arms that weren't hers either, Léon. I grew up missing something. I was bruised by the absence. That's why I want us to be together tonight, you and Joséphine and me.

Your little aunts, on the other hand, were treated with more indulgence. People took an interest in them. They had their photographs taken all the time; there were albums full of pictures. My parents stored the photos away carefully as if they never wanted to lose them. They collected everything: the girls' drawings, the ribbons they wore in their hair. They were entranced by the way the two resembled each other so closely, the pale grace of their faces, their green eyes, their chestnut, curly hair.

I thought they looked like two china dolls; they went everywhere together, even to the toilet. There was no place for me in their games, I didn't count, I was invisible. I was twelve and they were seven, the same age that you are now. They didn't talk to me, they said things *about* me: he smells bad. His sweater's ugly. He's put his finger up his nose. He has spots on his forehead. And on his nose. It's because his fingers are dirty. Luckily your grandfather was a pharmacist and he made me a special cream and the spots went away. My sisters were cruel sometimes; they said having a brother was pointless, they'd rather have a little dog.

One morning, one of my sisters didn't wake up.

And our whole family imploded.

Eighty Centimes

After going round to my father's, I came home to silence. The house was empty. You two were sleeping at your mother's. I didn't switch on any lights, I sat there in the darkness of the sitting room for a long time. I smoked a lot. No tears would come. I don't think I felt sad. Or angry. That was one particular fear I didn't have.

His disease didn't manifest itself as pain, but as immense hypocrisy. The tumour had spread beyond the colon to the lymph nodes and there were metastases on his liver. He might yet live.

I'll tell you that you have the right not to fight this, Papa, I would forgive you, we would all forgive you if, instead of indulging in useless, unavoidable suffering you'd rather spend a few days on a yacht on Lake Como, drive through Provence in a Bentley, drink a 1961 or a 1990 Château Pétrus, or laugh with my children, with Anna, with the living, or look at the photos of Anne for one last time. We would forgive you if you'd rather remember, believe in silly things, in reconciliation, in forgiveness.

I lit yet another cigarette, smiling, and I remembered the only time the two of us had had dinner on our own.

It was at the *Café de la Gare*.

His expression had been serious, and the watery green of his eyes was troubled. We had eaten our celeriac remoulade in silence, then he slowly wiped his lips on the rough cotton of his white napkin and began to speak.

I've received a letter from a man called Monsieur V. He says his daughter spent a night with a boy.

I blushed. If I hadn't already finished my starter, I'd have choked.

He says you were that boy, that it happened in England this summer, that she's only fourteen and it's an outrage. He says that if you try to see her again, to write to her, or phone her, if you even try to *think* about her for just one second he'll press charges against me for corruption of a minor.

You?

Me. I'm responsible for you until you come of age. So you are going to write to that gentleman and promise to do everything he says.

Here's eighty centimes for the stamp.

This was the mid-eighties. I was just fifteen, and very much in love with Patricia. She was small, with chestnut hair, big grey eyes, the colour of a rainy sky, and a huge smile. Our first time was tentative; it took us by surprise: there was laughter, tears, dry mouths. And now this stab to my heart. And eighty centimes, the price of my cowardice as I stood on the verge of manhood.

Aren't you going to ask if it was good, Papa? Aren't you going to welcome me into your grown-up world of giants? Aren't you going to open your arms to me in celebration?

I was leaving childhood by the back door, a door marked shame.

No, I am not going to ask if it was good. I don't want to know the details. It doesn't exist.

That was the evening when I lost you, Papa, when our weaknesses got the better of us. That evening, when my orphaned adolescence began.

After that, I watched you concentrate on cutting up your steak and chewing it. You put a lot of mustard on it. I didn't feel hungry any more, I wasn't hungry for a rare steak, or for your love. And each time you swallowed, it seemed to me that you were swallowing what little good there was left in my life, morsel by

35

morsel. I felt desperately empty that evening. And, ever since, not one of your glances or gestures, not one of the things you have said to me, has managed to soothe my suffering.

As I ground out my cigarette, the tears began to flow. At long last I was weeping for my father. The father I'd lost in a station brasserie. The father I'd dreamed of so often, imagining what would have become of us, all of us, if he had opened his arms to me that evening. If he'd talked to me, man to man. If he'd asked: Do you love her? Come on. Come on, get up, I'll drive you to her, and if her father tries to mess us around, I'll throw a little bottle of propionic acid in his face. Seriously! Come on, let's go.

Lost in these reveries, I laughed. I laughed.

Six Hundred And Fifty Francs
Seventy Centimes

The funeral was to take place at eleven on a Tuesday morning. Although my parents had said it would be a small, private ceremony, the church was full. As well as cousins, uncles and aunts, neighbours, and acquaintances, much of the congregation also consisted of the female customers of the Lapchin pharmacy, a whole crowd of them who had come in support of the man who had so often saved them from shame; from a gravy stain, the ravages of moths, tarnished silverware, or painful boils. They were grieving for my father's grief. My mother wanted it all to be over and done with, she wanted everything to disappear. The body. The emotion. She hadn't been able to understand the bill for six hundred and fifty francs seventy centimes – the cost of preserving the body of 'a child under twelve'.

She's dead, she's dead, she kept repeating, why on earth do we need to preserve her? You can't preserve a dead child, the body rots away. Everything rots away, everyone who loved her.

To keep the situation as calm as possible, my father had thought it advisable to choose the coffin alone (the child sizes began at one metre). It was made of poplar wood, eighteen millimetres thick. At the cemetery it started to rain and the ladies' hairstyles were ruined. Their tears turned black, blue, green, brown, orange and violet; every colour on the Rimmel palette. Their faces looked like children's drawings: scrawny trees, spiders' webs, sunbeams, blue rain, black ears of wheat. There were a few smiles, and some laughter, and what was supposed to be sad became light and graceful, like a little girl's soul. My sister had died in her sleep, and neither the family doctor nor the coroner could say why. Perhaps she no longer liked her half-life; perhaps she had realised that she was only one wing in a pair of two, condemned always to fly in circles.

After the funeral, everyone came back to our house. It looked like a scene from a Fellini film. The women with their rainbow-coloured faces. The grey, thin men, drenched by the rain. They drank, they nibbled on petit-fours from the Montois bakery, the champagne loosened their tongues, brought them closer together.

Isn't it sad, a little girl dying like that. Just seven years old, imagine that. Parents should never have to bury their children. And what about her sister? The twin? That's Anne, isn't it? No, Anne is the one who didn't wake up. The other twin is called Anna. How is she taking it? They're so alike. It's terrible, all her life her face will remind her of her sister's absence.

It wasn't generally known that when my mother had gone to wake them that fateful morning it had taken her several minutes to distinguish which twin was dead; they wore identical pyjamas, they had the same pearly fingernails, the same chestnut curls. It was during those minutes of uncertainty that the full horror of her life had overwhelmed her.

She left us the evening of the funeral. She abandoned us, in our big house, in our blue kitchen, among the empty glasses, the full ashtrays, the bottles of champagne and spirits, the boxes from the Montois bakery, the shoeboxes like little cardboard coffins full of photographs of our dead little sister. My mother left us as though we were nothing more than dirty dishes piled up in the sink, dirty washing in a laundry basket; she no longer had the strength, she couldn't take any more. My father tried to talk to her, to make a gesture.

It's over, André, it's over, I'm sorry, but you . . . no. No, don't say another word, please.

She took some things with her. Her books by Sagan. She stroked my cheek, planted a kiss on the forehead of

39

the surviving twin, who had not shed a tear or said a word since her double hadn't woken up.

Our mother was leaving.

And that was it.

She closed the front door carefully behind her, as if she wanted the last sound she made to be a gentle one.

Then our father asked us to come and sit beside him, on one of the Louis XV-style armchairs in the sitting room that our mother had had re-upholstered in a psychedelic orange fabric that was fashionable at the time. He held us close. He sobbed quietly. This show of weakness was too much for me and I suddenly began to hit him. I couldn't stop. He didn't try to dodge my fists. He did nothing at all. I had the fleeting impression that, as the tears overcame him, he was glad of my blows.

One Thousand Eight Hundred And
Seventy Billion Euros

But you know all about the bloody mess we're in, Antoine. Not a day goes by without another fucking tax. They pick your pocket. They pick your pants. Just like that, as if it's nothing. They worm their way in. They sit down at your dinner table. It's like me going up to someone and eating off their plate just because mine is empty. You wait and see, Antoine, soon they'll go and tax handsome men for putting ugly ones in the shade, and fat men, well, they shit more than others. No more bog roll, no more water. They eat more. They take up more room. Then they'll tax thin guys too, because they don't eat enough, they don't *consume* enough. And if people were taxed for being a dumb-ass, the taxman would get billions. Bloody billions. What's going on, eh? They don't tax civil servants, taxis, diesel, they definitely don't tax the salaries of our MPs, the flights they take, their train tickets, they get all that for free. No, we're the dumb ones. We're totally fucked. Thieving industrialists with their laboratories, they never end up in jail. And the guys who design speed traps. Not one of them would think of inventing something nice instead, like a pill to cure human misery. Or sadness. And what are we supposed to do? Lie down in the road? Strike? Not pay our taxes? Blockade planes? Hijack trains? When you get down to it, only in China could one guy stop a whole column of tanks. We're just spare pricks. We're one thousand eight hundred and seventy billion euros in debt. And we're not doing a single thing about it. We bawl and we yell and not a sound comes out. Not one fart. It's driving me crazy. Well, fuck it! Come on, Antoine, let's have a drink.

When FFF ranted on, he was like that grumpy old actor, Jean Gabin. All the same, even though he made me smile, I did share some of his anger. But, with me, none of the words or tears would come out. I never dared. I have never dared. I'm the type who bottles everything up. The type who doesn't say a word when a taxi driver takes the longest route, or when an old lady – under the pretext that she's an old lady – jumps the queue and screws me over, just like the taxi driver did.

The source of my cowardice is in this pent-up anger. I know forgiveness has never been a fundamental human quality; you have to fight, dare to be an animal, bite, defend yourself – or accept that you will disappear.

Sometimes I think about disappearing.

Since I had no urgent business, we went for a drink in the middle of the afternoon.

Our mothers are the authors of our lives, you know. The day FFF's mother opened a can of ravioli and found the fluorescent pink finger of a household glove, she passed out, and her son came running, thinking she was dead – ever since that day she mapped out his path in life. In spite of him.

If we don't watch out, he said, there'll be shit in our chocolate cake one of these days. Or horsemeat in beef lasagne.

After studying to be an engineer, FFF became a food safety consultant, while I established myself as an insurance expert after three years of studying law and an intensive course on motor engineering. FFF was a crusader, and history has proved him right, what with mad cow disease, dioxin-contaminated chicken, foot-and-mouth disease, bird flu and E. coli. He once had great dreams for the world, but I'll leave you to imagine what the world would choose between a dream and a twenty-euro note. He worked freelance, while I worked for two large insurance companies, and we shared offices; later, we recruited a part-time secretary. And sometimes we went for a drink in the middle of the afternoon.

The waiter had brought our beers. FFF took a long gulp, looking at me strangely, as if it wasn't really him, and wasn't really me, and then in the buzz of the café, as some people sighed and other people laughed, he murmured: Did you ever feel like going completely berserk?

Two Coffee Tokens

At the age of eighteen, I tried to meet girls.

I dreamed of a great, tragic love story. Something that would prove my mother and father wrong, something that would prove everyone wrong who, by leaving, had destroyed the lives of others, leaving bodies in their wake.

I dreamed of a brief but infinite love.

At the ice rink I noticed a prettily dressed blonde. Her virtuoso displays on the ice produced an illusion of lightness. I thought of Ali MacGraw, who also went skating, who loved Mozart, the Beatles and me. My lips were blue and my fingers were numb. All the same, I was smoking with a casual air, borrowing all the mannerisms that had made my mother look so confident and seductive. I also put my mind to blowing virtuoso smoke rings. She seemed only to notice me after she'd done twenty-seven laps of the rink. Later, of course, I learned that women never reveal everything at first. They keep things up their sleeve. It's the men who are ravenous.

Each time she went round after that, she smiled at me; on her fiftieth lap, her skates scraped across the ice, sending two wings of frost flying out behind her. She stopped right in front of me. Her beauty came from movement. But it was too late to go back now. She had already left the rink to join me, so I bought two coffee tokens.

Five minutes later we were outside in the sun, with our coffees; a few minutes later, our tongues were entangled, a blend of Mocha and Java; hers was incredibly soft, her mouth was warm, her fingers damp, and I abandoned my desire for a tragic love story, a brief but infinite love, because suddenly I wanted the weight of flesh. I wanted the things that make men go mad. That make them assassins. I slipped my hand under her sweater, and she didn't stop me. Her back. Her concave spine. The texture of her skin. Her beauty spots. The bra carving out the shape of her breasts. I struggled to unhook it. My fingers worked hard. Suddenly she laughed. *It's at the front, silly!* I didn't have a big brother, twin sisters, a father or even a mother who would teach me those secrets, show me how to be strong and forceful, a man who would take what he wanted. I ran away and she didn't call me back.

Can you imagine that, Léon? I didn't even tell her my name.

After that I was with Djamila for a while. I'd met her at FFF's eighteenth birthday. We used to meet in my dorms (she was studying literature, I was studying law), and we didn't talk much, our vocabulary was action, it was love and making love, clawing and crying out. We'd been deprived for so long. There was no tenderness or shame, it was magnificent. The kind of thing that gives men an erection: the darkness, the way we fell. She taught me all those acts that make a woman go dizzy with pleasure. I'd never before smelt the musky darkness of those blind alleys, I'd never seen the rose, the diamond of flesh, I'd never been drunk with that kind of intoxication. We were flesh and blood, and it felt good. We burned off our dead skin, our small humanity, our childhood suffering. And when, one morning, exhausted by the vanity of our trysts, we parted, there was no sadness between us, only a gentle look, and the stirrings of goodwill. We said goodbye with a handshake and a few choice phrases. 'Good luck in life.' 'Good luck to you, too.' I think I told her, 'Be happy.' She smiled and said, 'Right, well, goodbye.' And then she was gone.

Later I found a book by Modiano that she had left

behind. I still have it. It's the only photo I have of her. And then there were other 'wonderful nights that pass by'.* Among them was your Mama, Léon: Nathalie.

When I met her, I thought I had found love.

---

* Alfred de Musset, *Les Caprices de Marianne*.

Two Times Three Hundred Francs

On the advice of the woman who was to become his wife, and because she worked for a dentist — You can trust me, Monsieur André, I know about these things — our father sent us to see a psychologist.

Since the disappearance of our mother and the death of our sister, Anna had not said a word, and I was still furious with my father. I hadn't hit him again but I'd taken to punching the walls of my bedroom, powerful blows that bruised my hands. I also kicked my bike and sometimes I threw pebbles at windows or dashed things to the ground so that they broke: their framed black-and-white wedding photograph, the braces I wore on my teeth, my watch. I wanted time to stand still, preserving them as they were for ever, their fresh faces, the slight perfume they gave off, the colour of their eyes, the exact pink of their lips. I dreaded that moment of horror that came to me day after day, the

49

end of the world in miniature: the fear that my sense of them might disappear entirely and I would have nothing left, nothing but an abstraction, not one bit of flesh. Nothing at all.

The psychologist wasn't too bad. For two times three hundred francs he made Anna and me take a series of tests and fill in questionnaires designed to evaluate separation anxiety and the anguish of mourning. He asked us to draw pictures so he could decipher our sorrow, and do exercises to help him assess our level of anger – me, especially. He asked one hundred questions to get to the heart of our denial. I emerged with a pre-scription for antidepressants, half a 5mg Valium tablet every evening, plus two visits to him each week. These things take time, he said.

My anger was pushed down into my stomach, along with the tablets, and never re-emerged.

My sister was sent to a speech therapist, again twice a week, and an osteopath to be on the safe side, so he could stimulate her oral nerve, her pterygoid muscles and the hollow depression under her tongue.

When Anna went to her specialist for the first time, I went with her. We had barely left the house when she took my hand – her little hand in my large one – and my heart lifted. All those years neither she nor Anne had ever touched or embraced me. They were the whole world to each other, except for the tenderness shared between them and my mother, the way she soothed their fears with her caresses.

I stopped to look at my sister. She had raised her lovely green eyes to mine and was smiling at me. She was just seven years old. I hadn't realised how beautiful she was. Her little hand squeezed mine harder, and in that moment I knew we were going to be friends.

I glad you my.

She said only one word out of every two.

Five Hundred And Sixty Euros

Not so long ago I was getting threats. Not directly. It wasn't like some film where a gangster comes up to you clenching his fist: Watch out, because next time . . . No. It was minor stuff. Scratches on my car. Shit – dog shit, I suppose – through the letter box at the office. Graffiti on the door, a skull, that sort of thing. I had my suspicions who was behind it, but there was nothing I could do. FFF insisted on going to the police station with me to lodge a complaint.

We won't be looking into it, Monsieur, the sergeant told me; we have a backlog of eight hundred complaints that haven't been dealt with, we've put CCTV cameras all over the place and we still can't catch these graffiti artists and petty thieves. Crime is evolving. It's slippery and sly. We're always on the back foot, and when we do arrive on the scene we just get abuse and stones thrown at us. So no, we won't be doing a DNA test on the dog shit you mentioned. This isn't *Miami Vice*, it's a local police station, the dustbin of human misfortune, sir. Stolen tyres, dismantled scooters, battered women, drunken scuffles, kids who've been burned by a joint. I used to like the idea of being a guardian of the peace – imagine that, *a guardian of the peace* – but it's a war zone out there, I'm not a guardian of anything and all my dreams have been shattered. They're all gone, the lot of them. But if you still want to lodge a complaint, I can't stop you. I'll call a trainee to fill in the forms. It'll take some time because our computer's broken.

I had filed a report on a case of alleged whiplash: someone had run into a man's car while he was waiting at a red light. Besides the damage to the rear of his car, he was complaining of pain at the back of his neck. Good old whiplash. My findings were as follows: temporary incapacity for work (not that he stopped working) – seven days; physical pain on a scale of one to seven – two; damage to physical and psychological well-being – 2 per cent. This amounted to a claim for seven thousand euros. The victim had a 1998 Volvo S70. In this model, the three-point seat belt locks immediately on impact, there is no stretch or give there, so the body is not thrown forwards before being violently pulled back by the tension of the belt. The ergonomic design of the headrest leaves practically no space between it and the driver's head. Very well, so the man was in some pain, but as my job didn't allow any room for compassion, I had decided to check up on him by engaging a private detective who charged seventy euros an hour. After two four-hour periods of observation he brought me some photographs that clearly showed my whiplash victim at the Macumba Club, dancing with two young women. He was distinctly visible, his head wagging excitedly, a break-dance virtuoso. The photos were very good. I turned down his claim for compensation and got dog shit in return.

Too bad. In the end, I didn't lodge a complaint.

Back home, I poured myself a large glass of wine. Inside I was seething, my anger rumbling inside my body. The Valium of my teenage years had suppressed it, so that it lay in wait in my guts, filling me up, my own little hermit crab. I'd have liked to be strong, to go and punch the virtuoso break-dancer in the face, break his teeth, wring his neck, stuff his dog shit down his throat, the shit of all the people who fuck up our lives. Stealthily, over the course of time. The whole risky process ending with a perfect corpse.

The sod who carves you up on the road.

The fishmonger who swears that you gave him a ten-euro note, not a twenty.

The corked wine you paid too much for.

Dearest Nathalie, the first time she put the knife in.

But I couldn't do it. I couldn't bring myself to. When someone hurt me I would always blame myself. And so I smoked and drank a lot that night, in the silence of my apartment. I'd have been glad to have had you there, you and Joséphine. I'd have asked for forgiveness, and I, in turn, would have forgiven the chemist for injecting me with his weakness. But forgiveness isn't in our nature, you know that.

The alcohol put my anger to sleep. My innate cowardice had won again.

That night.

All My Marbles

I understand why you don't talk to me much. I know your pain. I was the same at your age, and I still am today. I used to punch my pillow and bite my nails until my fingers bled. I swapped all my marbles for a few of the really large ones, taws or boulders they were called, and threw them at the windows of cars and houses; I liked the sound they made. I felt the same way you do. I was afraid. I was afraid, the way you're afraid. One day of grief can erase a thousand days of happiness. It isn't fair. You and I should have talked more, should have known each other better. You're smart, you're intelligent. You know, I once asked my father why does it rain. He looked at the sky and shrugged, as though I'd asked a stupid question. He was a chemist, I know he knew about such things, and the hows and whys of storms and tides as well. But he didn't tell me the answer. I expect he was too busy thinking about something else, or the question made me sound as if I was begging for love, and that terrified him. It's a difficult question, Léon. I found out the answer so I'd be ready for the day when you'd ask me. But you never did.

We stayed with our father, your aunt and I. He didn't even know how to make an omelette or chocolate mousse, he didn't know how to braid Anna's hair, or even how to work the washing machine. At first, he got a cleaning lady, and then he took a wife to keep house for us all. He and I didn't talk much, no more than you and I do.

I know that when we're sad we never turn to the people who might be able to comfort us. And that makes us even sadder. We think we came into the world because our parents loved each other, and then we discover they didn't want us enough to stay with us. Growing up means understanding that no one is loved as much as that. It's painful. I'm sad about Mama too, sad that we're not a family any more, that it turned out the way it did, sad to see that nothing ever lasts. That love is cowardly too. If only you knew how tired I feel, Léon, how sad I am tonight because of this horrible thing, because of what I'm going to do.

So. When water evaporates in the sun, passing from a liquid to a gaseous state, it becomes lighter than air, it flies away and forms clouds. And when the clouds pass over cooler zones, the water condenses, returning to its liquid state. That's why it rains.

That's the answer, Léon.

But there's another answer, one I'd have loved to give you, because I think it's better. It comes from the Maori culture. When the world was created, the Maoris say, Ranginui and Papatuanuku – or Rangi and Papa – lived permanently intertwined, condemning their children to grow up between them in a dark and cramped space. Their son Tane didn't like that, so one day he lay on his back and pushed Papa with his arms, and Rangi with his feet, until they separated.

Ranginui became the Sky Father. Papatuanuku became the Earth Mother. And rain is the terrible grief that Rangi felt at that separation.

Two Balls

I remember our delight the day you were born. You arrived three years after Joséphine. Nathalie's second pregnancy, it seemed, had been a second happy one. In the last three months she stopped going out in the afternoons, preferring the calm, cool peace of our home. In the last few weeks, she decided to repaint the kitchen, and then the bedrooms. We looked like the perfect young family, something out of a magazine, in shades of marshmallow pink. There are photos from that time of Joséphine placing cuddly toys in the cot, ready for her little brother. Others show her hugging her mother's big tummy. Joséphine drawing and painting pictures, getting lots of welcome presents ready. Joséphine doing a handstand in the sitting room. Playing at being a mummy with a doll. Joséphine is beautiful. Nathalie is planting hyacinth bulbs in our little garden. Nathalie laughing, displaying her breasts, which are three times their usual size. Nathalie blowing me a kiss. In our kitchen, my father is smiling, his wife is holding his hand; Nathalie had made sea bass baked in a thyme and salt crust, and the fish was overdone. We don't see the fish being cooked in the photographs. We don't see the insincere compliments: *The sea bass was just perfect*. We see our new car. We see me standing next to the new car, looking like an idiot. We see the Barbie tricycle. We see Joséphine and Nathalie in the bath. We see Anna and her husband Thomas in our little garden beside a wilting hyacinth. We don't see my mother. We don't see the lies. We don't see the baby that Nathalie hadn't wanted to keep a year earlier, because she wasn't sure she would always love me. We don't see that love of ours, brief and infinite, vast and tragic. We don't see the tears I would shed. The nights I spent on the sofa. The insomnia that plagued me. The trouble brewing at that time. The wild beast awakening.

We only saw happiness.

Five Euros Sixty-Seven

His laughter had left him. The green of his eyes had dissolved entirely into grey. The gentle touch of his hands was gone, like dead skin being sloughed off. Now and then a crown of sweat would appear on his forehead, burning like acid. He had already lost weight. His wife's lower lip trembled uncontrollably; it was a kind of tic, of terror, a cry that didn't want to come out. The sickness of one awoke the fear of the other. Within a few weeks, my father had gone completely grey. A little old man had moved in.

It's because of the pills they're giving him he's too weak his body is too weak for real chemotherapy that's what the oncologist said she's a good woman devoted to her job she really listens oh I cried so much Antoine you just can't imagine how much but it's better for him to be here with me than in hospital you see some terrible things in hospital and in his present state it's better that he sees pleasant things I put musicals on the DVD player for him they relax him and a musical usually has a happy ending it's full of hope.

My father's wife was gently foundering. He was floating in his lies. It's nothing. It's benign, it was diagnosed very early. There's nothing to worry about.

Her lower lip was panicking. I felt so sorry for her. I remembered how nasty Anna and I had been when she first moved into the house, filling our mother's cupboards with her things, occupying half the washbasin, taking the Cardinale books down to the cellar but leaving the Barjavels and Sagans where they were. Some evenings we used to hear her sobbing through the bedroom door. Her tears were our childish victories. When our father took us to one side and begged us to be nice to her we would run away, shouting: Never, never! We wanted her to be unhappy so she'd leave, we wanted her dead, we wanted her not to be there any more, we wanted there to be nothing left of her on the day our mother came back. But one woman stayed and the other never did come back.

After our mother left, our father took to drinking beer. In the evenings, in the blue kitchen, he would drink in silence until the tears came. Anna and I would sit on the stairs in our pyjamas, spying on him. Sometimes we cried too. And sometimes my sister's little hand slipped into mine. She would say: *Promise I wake*. Sometimes she said: *Did happen Anne not?* There were evenings when my father fell asleep at the kitchen table, his head on his plate. He wasn't there in the mornings when we woke up. We used to pass the Lapchin pharmacy before going to school to make sure he was there, that he was still alive, and there he would be, showing off to the lonely ladies, the widows, the women with stains to be removed, demonstrating his potions and how well they worked.

Then the silk blouse and the pretty breasts came into our lives. Our father stopped drinking and slept in his bed, not in the kitchen. She made him give up cigarettes. And chips, and charcuterie, and lamb. Palm oil and chocolate and full-cream milk. She hadn't known any other man and she wanted to keep this one for a long time. For ever, she said, smiling dreamily, in the early days; for ever, that was the most important thing.

For ever lasted nearly thirty years and ended in tears, sweat, piss and slobber. Ugliness always follows beauty. There is nothing lovely left.

I never had a child of my own but now that your father is ill I feel as if I have one it's a funny feeling you think you're doing these things for yourself as well so you won't be forgotten but I don't think that's true you're always alone and that's what makes me sad.

I opened three of the six cans of Leffe I'd brought with me, five euros sixty-seven centimes' worth, enough to give us a small buzz.

Oh you shouldn't have Antoine.

Yes, yes, that's good, said my father, considering the point we've reached.

And so we toasted each other. We drank to musicals. To metastases. To time beginning again. We drank to anything and everything.

Life was slipping through our fingers.

One Franc

I glad you my.

She had smiled when she said that to me. Her green eyes had shone. It must have been something beautiful, luminous. The baptism of our friendship. A bond between survivors that would never break. I am glad that my doctor. No. I am glad that you are with me. No, no. I am glad that you are my brother. Yes, yes, yes. She had looked at me, overwhelmed. Seven years of polite indifference were erased and we became friends, we were indispensable to each other. The absence of Anne and our mother brought us together. We would go through childhood moored to one another, we would protect each other, she would no longer be frightened and I would no longer feel cold.

I am glad that you are my brother.

I am happy that you are my sister, Anna.

She had given me the key to the code; I was the only

one who understood it. I had no need, as others did, to advance theories, to suggest missing words, to get angry. She spoke and I heard what her heart was saying. *Promise I wake*: I promise that I will wake up. *Did happen Anne not*: why did it happen to Anne and not me? *You we'll Mama*: do you think we'll see Mama again?

That day I was waiting for her to come out of her first session with the speech therapist. I had bought her one franc's worth of Malabar chewing gum at the bakery, five pieces coloured the same pink as her room. From the superiority of my twelve years, I was sure that if she chewed, munched, masticated, her missing words would come back to her. But they stayed where they were, imprisoned in our dead little sister's throat. Every other word. *Thanks I that stay this*, she had said, smiling, when I gave her the chewing gum. Thanks, but I think that I'll stay like this. I suddenly felt scared for her. How would she make friends, speaking in half-sentences? Would she ever have a handsome boyfriend? An attractive fiancé? How does the love story go when *I love you* comes out as *I you*? When *don't ever leave me* becomes *ever me*, and *come to my arms* is *come my*?

And how can you leave someone by saying *I love any more* instead of *I don't love you any more*?

That evening, when we got home, our father was waiting for us in the kitchen. He had bought a cheese tart from the Montois bakery, lettuce, walnuts from Le Vert Pré, and ice cream. He wanted us to eat together as a family for the first time since they had left us. Like a sort of communion. The rims of his eyes were red, the green irises already dimming to the colour of mud. He tried to make us smile. He talked about the summer, where would we like to go on holiday? Would we like to go sailing? Climbing? Abroad, perhaps, Mexico, Guatemala. Countries where even just saying the name felt like travel. Vanuatu. Zanzibar. Would you like some more cheese tart? It's good, not too fatty. The Montois bakery never puts too much butter in it. Did you know that butter melts at thirty degrees?

And when Anna finally opened her mouth, *This no, cheese won't them, who buy to in house, will shopping, not who we still family, that not I'd love*, he didn't understand her. So I squeezed my sister's hand under the table. We were on our own.

Two Hundred Euros More

'But you're not listening! I tell you it was as good as new.'

'New? It was from 1985!'

'Exactly. March '85. Bought brand new in Onnaing. Beautifully maintained. Not a scratch on it. Not one trace of rust, Monsieur. Not a mark.'

'A brand-new twenty-two-year-old car. I can understand why someone would want to steal it.'

'And very few kilometres on the clock. I took it to buy bread every morning. And for a nice drive every Sunday, except when it rained. That's all. Or no, I once had to take it to Paris when Yvette, that's my wife, had a thing with her heart. Marfan syndrome.'

'I'm sorry to hear that, Monsieur.'

'All the same, I think your offer of two thousand euros is pathetic.'

'One thousand eight hundred, Monsieur Grzesko-wiek.'

'Grzeskowiak.'

'Grzeskowiak. One thousand eight hundred euros, to which I have added another two hundred euros for the very reason that there were so few kilometres on the clock.'

'But what can I do with two thousand euros? I can't buy another new car at that price. I want my Fuego back. It was a GTS. Yellow.'

'I understand, but I'm not David Copperfield.'

'Who?'

'Never mind. He's a magician. What I am trying to tell you, Monsieur Grzeskowiek, I mean Grzeskowiak, is that I've offered you the maximum amount of compensation. I calculated it at the highest possible rate then added two hundred euros.'

'I was well brought up and I don't think I have ever been one to use coarse language, Monsieur. But you can stick your two thousand euros up your arse. My car was as good as new. Now I don't have a car, and I don't suppose I'll ever be able to buy another one. You're a useless, heartless loser. You're a pile of shit. A stinking pile of shit. People are suffering all around you and you do nothing. You just push them further into the shit. I hope you die a long and horrible death. Good evening, Monsieur.'

That was the story of my life.

Ten Numbers

I'd lost weight. I needed new trousers and shirts. You're not a student any more, you're *an expert*, you'd better look classy. FFF had been mocking me. So I went off to the Printemps department store one Saturday afternoon. There were crowds of people, women, children, queues everywhere for the cash desks and the fitting rooms. At last my turn came. I tried on the trousers. One pair would be all right if I got the hem altered. I emerged from my cubicle in the fitting room to look for a salesgirl. A woman was coming out of her cubicle at the same moment. She was wearing a tight-fitting white dress and couldn't do up the long zip at the back.

Our eyes met.

I felt it immediately. The thing that strikes men down. The serpent's spellbinding eye turned on its prey. I was paralysed. That gaze was the reason I was still alive; it traced the shape of an island with me at its centre.

Our eyes met and I had never felt so desired, so ardently desired that abandoning myself no longer seemed like an act of cowardice, but of love.

Our eyes met and my survival instinct told me to lose myself in her. It promised me dizzying heights, the kind of experiences that help a person overcome the disasters of childhood.

And so, for the first time in my life, I dared.

I stuck out my arm and did up her zip. My fingers were trembling, because they had never done such a thing before. Her skin was soft, a pale caramel. She didn't look at herself in the mirror, she looked at me. Me. Assessing herself in the tiny mirrors of my eyes, she turned in profile to me. Her right side, then her left. She stood there like a doe, adjusting the straps of the dress as she looked at her reflection in my eyes. Incredible. The girl and the dress. She smiled then, took hold of my sleeve, and led me into her cubicle. Once there, she raised her arms, undid the top of the zip, and pulled it halfway down her back. I went to help her again, responding to her gesture. With a wiggle of her shoulders and then her hips, she let the dress slip to the floor. It created a white ring at her feet, an engagement ring. She had pretty breasts. They were pale and heavy. A graceful body. She put on another dress, black this time, all the time watching me as I watched her. She was bewitching. Then she undressed again. She tried on a skirt, a pencil skirt in Prussian blue. I trembled as she twisted it around her waist. A whirlwind, in dizzying slow motion. She put her hands on her hips; our eyes locked. The serpent might bite me, but who cared? I was happy. Then she thanked me for helping her, in a lovely, rather serious voice.

I'm going to buy the black dress, and I think you should buy the dark green trousers.

She smiled. I looked down at the trousers with the too-long legs; I was a little boy aged twenty-five only just shedding my childhood skin. I should have done it then and there, but, in my family, we didn't do things in a hurry. We hadn't learned to elbow people out of the way and help ourselves. We waited for an invitation or, sometimes, a summons.

I returned to my cubicle, trembling, and sat down on the bench.

A moment later, a caramel-coloured hand and arm snaked through the folds of the curtain. The fingers dropped a little piece of paper. It had ten numbers on it. I quickly put my trousers back on, leaving all the other clothes in the fitting room.

I had just met Nathalie. Your Mama. But, of course, she had already left.

A Fortune

Our father sometimes gave us news of our mother.

She's all right. She's found a job. We've divorced.

Tears rose to Anna's eyes and mine began to sting. Divorced. The word claimed three casualties in one go. Mama. Childhood. Reconciliation. From now on my sister and I were going to have to grow up fast.

She's living in Bagnolet, near the Périphérique, she says she's happy in her job and she's made some friends. She's thinking of you.

When we her, Papa. I translated for Anna. When can we see her, Papa?

I don't know, Antoine. Not straightaway, she needs some time on her own. But she sees her friends and not us? I don't know, Antoine, don't ask me questions I don't know the answer to.

His gold wedding ring had left a red indentation on his finger, like the scar from a burn. I hoped with all my heart that it hurt, hurt him badly, I hoped that his finger would go rotten and fall off, that gangrene would spread to his arm and then his heart. We were to grow up without even the shadow of a mother; we were to grow up any which way. To turn into prickly brambles.

One Saturday, after our sessions with the speech therapist and the psychiatrist, Anna and I walked to the train station instead of returning home. We passed the Palace cinema, outside which was a huge poster of Edwige Fenech's breasts, advertising the latest film. We went into the draughty station concourse. I shielded Anna from several pairs of wandering, pathetic hands, the hands of people who might steal children; I hadn't forgotten the tragic tale of the Lindbergh case. We then stood at the counter, waiting for the answer to our question.

Cambrai to Bagnolet, change at Douai, at the Gare du Nord take the number 26 to the Porte de Bagnolet. Then let your little legs do the rest. Do you have a family railcard? No. Then that'll be two hundred and twenty-five francs for a return ticket. Each.

Two hundred and twenty-five francs was a fortune: the cost of ten or eleven Sagan books, four hundred and fifty Mars bars, fifty-five packets of unfiltered Gitanes. Anna's fingers felt like tears in my hand.

Well, kids, have you made up your mind? Other

people are waiting, you know. You're not on your own here. But that's just it, Madame, we *are* on our own.

We left shamefaced, upset, grubby. We took the long way home, avoiding the Lapchin pharmacy, the Montois bakery, Le Vert Pré, avoiding all those places where we'd seen our parents together, pretending to be happy.

Back at home, I made my little sister a snack. A banana sprinkled with brown sugar and a glass of lemonade: everything was yellow. Ever since the day when Anne hadn't woken up, Anna had rejected the colour pink. I swore to her, that day, that I would find the money for us to go and see our mother. *Do think can it.* I don't know if I can do it, Anna. I'll steal it if I have to, I'll kill if I have to.

It was the promise of a coward, I know.

Two Euros Sixty Centimes

There would be flying cars. We'd be able to race on the backs of fishes. Solar energy would replace oil. Robots would do the jobs people thought they were above now. Emptying rubbish bins, picking up dog shit, mopping up vomit. And sex work, in the darkness of alleyways, in densely overgrown parks, would also be done by robots instead of desperate women and young girls. There'd be no more violence. Everyone would own a computer. No one would be lonely. We'd all have mobile phones, we'd call people who were in trouble, we'd save them, we'd bring them back to life. I had grown up believing there would be water in Africa, aspirin and antibiotics. Electricity would do nothing more harmful than give the world light – no one would connect it to a man's testicles in the yellow sands of the desert. We'd go on holiday to the Moon, Mars, Jupiter; we'd fly round Saturn. We'd begin to dream of teleportation.

Plastic hearts would save human hearts. We'd be able to repair the body. We'd have extras, spare body parts. We would live in perfect health for a hundred and twenty, a hundred and thirty years. The words Alzheimer's and cancer would fall out of use; they'd be like hieroglyphs. We'd be happy. We were all going to be happy. And the year 2000 came upon us.

Our childhood dreams would surely be realised one day, but we were adults now. Money hadn't solved anything. Shadows were falling. Starving people had butchered an animal outside a farm in Saint-Antonin, in the Tarn-et-Garonne; they left its guts but took away two hundred and twenty kilos of meat. Elsewhere chickens, turkeys and ducks were stolen. Foxes were blamed. Wolves were blamed. Men are called by strange names when they are hungry. A ton of potatoes was dug up. Diesel was siphoned off. Red wine. Flowerpots disappeared, as did fences and lawnmowers. Rusting mopeds. Bolts, cables, chains. Trains were derailed, sheet metal cut through live bodies, decapitated pretty heads. Anger growled, wild beasts awakened. Whole families went to hypermarkets to eat, throwing the empty packaging on the floor, shitting in the car park. At Lyon-Part-Dieu, four night watchmen beat a homeless man to death for stealing a beer. Insurance companies were swindled, and dog shit was put through my letterbox. I saw an elegant grandfather and his grand-daughter, dressed in Bonpoint, steal a packet of biscuits costing two euros sixty centimes from the Relais H at Lille station. Just two euros sixty centimes. Women begged in the streets, carrying children made drowsy with codeine syrup. Drinking water was cut off if you couldn't pay the rent. In Bagnolet, my mother was robbed and we didn't even know.

No one had warned me that the people who love you might also kill you.

Shadows were falling, and the darkness frightened me.

Twenty Or Twenty-Five Francs

We didn't go to Zanzibar or Mexico. There was no sailing trip, no visit to the seaside.

That first summer without Mama and Anne, our father sent us for one month to a summer camp in Bourg-d'Oisans, a pretty place in the south-east of France, 1,900 metres above sea level. *Does mean will near sky Mama*. No, Anna, it doesn't mean we will be near the sky and Mama, it means we're completely lost.

There were about a hundred children there and a dozen monitors looking after us. Open-air activities. Ball games. Short climbing expeditions. Abseiling for the bolder kids. Hiking, long walks to Lake Lauvitel. Paddling in the water. Laughter, splashing about. Grazed knees. First kisses, exchanged in secret, sometimes under water. Clumsy caresses. We looked at the peak of La Meije with fear. Dreamed of escape, of a wind that would carry us to Bagnolet. The purity of the air lent us wings. Kids shouted, their cries rose up and scared the birds. At lunchtime we had picnics amid the picture-postcard scenery of Les Écrins national park. Blue skies, lush green grass, red pheasant's eye, white lilies, yellow shell moths. In the evenings we had dinner in the camp, sitting around a blazing fire. The monitors played the guitar, we sang simple songs that we'd heard again and again on the car radio, the female monitors danced, their skin shining, while the boys, who barely had hair in their armpits, placed stupid bets: twenty or twenty-five francs that I get a feel of Lolo, the mono, with the big tits. And when it was time for us to go off to our tents for the night, to do battle with mosquitoes and watch out for snakes, Anna and I stayed together.

On the day we arrived, I'd told the supervisors about our story and our fear of being separated. I'd explained Anna's mutilated language, and how she was being teased at school – that's the girl who talks like a baby, the girl who'll get fat because she eats so many of her own words, the girl who can't even count properly. The monster! The monster! Children could be as violently cruel as fathers. Childhood was so short it flew away the moment you opened your arms to embrace it, the moment you made the mistake of think-ing it would come back of its own accord. Hanging on to your share of childhood was the only way to stay alive. The director of the camp understood. He found a small tent for Anna and me, where we could whisper while the others had to be silent once the lights were out. She put her head on my shoulder; outside, the night had a cold, keen edge, and we clung to each other, *Tell about*, she whispered to me. And I told her about our mother, the wonderful aroma of menthol, the amazing chocolate mousse she sometimes made, the cheese soufflés that often sank in the middle, the rice she'd overcook, the empty fridge, the beers drunk in sadness. *Because was sorry*. Because she was so unhappy. Yes, she was unhappy. Then Anna talked about Anne, and we smiled.

Anne had known when Anna needed to go to the toilet even before Anna knew it herself, and Anna had known that Anne would have a tummy pain before she even felt it, or that Anne would want to read a certain book, or wear a certain dress.

I was the only one who understood.

That summer, I asked one of the female monitors to teach me how to braid hair: in the Egyptian style, plaited with three strands, with five strands. I made Anna all kinds of chestnut-coloured crowns. My sister was beautiful. A boy her own age gently approached us, a likeable young lad. She blushed a delicate pink and looked at me proudly, already lost.

One day we visited the Botanic Gardens on the Lautaret Pass. While we were in the Arctic rock garden, this boy plucked a cotton-grass flower and gave it to Anna when no one was looking. It was a strange flower, a stem with fluffy white hairs on top. A miniature princess of the tundra, a kind of angel. And my sister replied with a complete phrase: *Thanks*. There was a lovely smile on the boy's face when he said in turn: *I you pretty*. I think you are pretty.

We were no longer alone in the world. From that moment on we had Thomas.

Ninety-Four Centimes

The tablets hadn't worked. My father had lost even more weight. His grey skin had turned a waxen yellow, like the colour of a church candle. Of a faded prayer. The pain was more muted now, but it came out bleeding from his anus and his throat, as if he'd swallowed marbles of ground glass. This made it difficult for him to breathe. His hands shook, so that sometimes he lost his grip on the ninety-four-centime bottle, and the spilt beer looked like a piss stain on his trousers. Ugliness won the day. His clothes, from now on mainly empty, were an insult to his shrivelled body. I brought him three new suits in three different sizes, which made him look even smaller. He must keep his dignity, I murmured, horrified. The cruelty of his disease knew no bounds.

André listen to your son he's brought you some clothes so you'll look smart he's always looked smart your father has even wearing his white coat in fact I think I had a crush on his white coat when he was work-ing at the Lapchin pharmacy anyone would have taken him for an important doctor I'm sure you remember Lapchin and how brilliant and funny your father was all of the ladies were mad about him and when your poor mother left we all wondered whether he'd replace her one day you and Anna were so young it wouldn't have been right for the two of you to grow up without a mother no one can do that and your little sister oh my God your little sister and then I was the one he chose I don't know why I really don't know why.

You were kind, my father said faintly.

Kind. I smiled. Kindness isn't love. Kindness is com-panionship. A walk together lasting thirty years, at the most. I am convinced that my father never really loved anyone, and among all the other misfortunes that he unloaded on me perhaps this was another: his inability to love. His greatest weakness. Our greatest weakness from that point on.

Papa, if you want to go yachting on Lake Como or drive a Bentley through Provence, if you want to drink a 1961 or a 1990 Château Pétrus, then this is the time. This is the time when you owe me an explanation, when you owe us an explanation. You have a right to choose something that won't last, you have a right to choose lightness of heart, to do as you want, to indulge yourself – you don't have the right to regret any more.

My father's wife moved away. She was crying. She didn't want him to see her grief, the fear of finding herself alone the following day, maybe early the next morning; her terror of suddenly having nothing.

That's the hardest part Antoine the idea of being alone not knowing what's going to happen in fifteen minutes' time in five minutes' time or even in one minute's time when he asks me for a stuffed tomato or a bowl to spit into and when he coughs it hurts his throat so much yet I feel so very alive oh I'm so sad.

The collateral damage of illness is impossible to calculate.

If you want to look at the photograph albums of the twins and see Anne again, now's the time, Papa. He laid his rust-coloured hand on my arm, struggling for breath. A moment passed. Yes. There's one thing I'd like. I'd like to take you to see that little English girl, her name was Patricia, wasn't it? And if her father kicks up a fuss I have a little bottle of propionic acid with me. Really. His smile was like a grimace. A small victory. I was crying.

Why do we only meet those we've missed just as we're losing them?

Zero

It was twelve days before I called Nathalie. Every day I kept telling myself I'd call her soon, I'd call her tomorrow.

Years earlier, when we were at a summer camp in l'Alpe-d'Huez, I had finally received the letter I was so eagerly awaiting. The letter from Amandine P*. We were just sixteen, we'd pouted at each other, exchanged meaningful looks – amusing, childish nonsense. Before the holidays I'd asked if she would go out with me, and at last her reply had arrived. I slipped the envelope into one of my pockets, waiting for the best moment to open it and savour its words, because of course it was a love letter, and you don't spoil a love letter by reading it when you're with other people. I waited for a day, two days; a whole week passed. At night I breathed in the perfume of the letter, dreaming of Amandine's words. When my fingers brushed the envelope my heart gently swelled, and I was happy, I was waiting.

One morning, we had climbed to the mountain refuge above the Fare valley, the Alpette, to go hiking and visit the Lac du Milieu and the Lac de la Fare. It had rained the previous night and the air was surprisingly mild, like a warm caress. The sky looked astonishing. Two eagles were flying very high up, as if in slow motion. Anna and Thomas were walking ahead of me, laughing, but I wasn't listening. It was the perfect moment. So I opened the envelope, and unfolded the sheet of paper, trembling.

No. That was all she had written. NO. No, I will not go out with you, no, I don't like you enough, said her parsimonious pen. I went pale. I was walking quite fast and one of the monitors looked at me with concern. It's the altitude, I said. Then the blood began to boil in my veins again, and I started to smile. Cowardice some-times takes strange forms, you know. Mine had just given me twenty days of happiness dreaming of the nice things that Amandine P* would say, and her single-word answer couldn't take that away from me.

I waited twelve days to call Nathalie and I experi-enced the same happiness. I felt the same fear too, when she answered the phone. But this time the answer was yes. Yes. But you took your time, didn't you? Yes. I'd like to see you again. A coffee, if you like. Yes. Or a glass of

Shiraz. That's what I'd prefer. Australian, then, it's stronger and more tannic. You're right, it goes well with red meat. Red meat is perfect. Yes, dinner then, that's fine by me. I'd like to do that. So would I. This evening. Your black dress. Your green trousers. Oh, so you didn't buy them in the end. I . . . er, no, I didn't. I ran after you but I couldn't find you. And you missed me too.

She laughed. Her laughter was like a bright light.

We didn't kiss after dinner. Neither of us went back to the other's place. She was in the middle of a break-up with some random guy. She didn't want us to begin amid difficulties and unpleasantness. She wanted to start again. She wanted a clean slate.

That's something all men dream of. It's our misfortune that we only find out what's been written on it at the end.

Four Ninety-Nine

Your mother left that guy, and we saw each other again as soon as possible. We were stupidly in love. Like twelve-year-olds. We would not leave each other's side, even to go to the toilet. You've never seen us like that: we fed each other, we drank from the same glass, we swapped T-shirts, toothbrushes. I know, you can hardly imagine it. Nor can I. I never saw my own parents being happy together, loving one another to the music of happiness. Never a kiss, never a loving look. Well, I've seen a little of that between my father and his wife, but by then it was already affection. The next stage. Your mother was beautiful, Léon, I used to wake up in the night just to look at her, to listen to her breathing. Men turned to look at her in the street, it made her laugh, and her laughter was luminous and attracted kind comments. And malicious ones too. At first I was torn between pride and jealousy, and then such words disappeared. I simply felt that I had been lucky, that I was the one she had chosen that day in the fitting room. I was the one she wanted to have children with, Joséphine and you; I was the one she wanted to drink Blood and Sand cocktails with in the bar of a hotel with an unpronounceable name in Mexico or some such place; I was the one she wanted to grow old with. I thought that she was offering me what she had refused to other men, but love makes you blind and deaf, it isolates you, harms you, and you don't notice until later.

We moved into a nice apartment near the main square, close to the offices I share with FFF. And then Joséphine came along; it wasn't quite the right moment, because Nathalie had just started her job with Decathlon a few months earlier, she had fought hard to get it and she was afraid she wouldn't be taken back after her maternity leave. But they did take her back. They waited for her. Everyone waited for her, everyone loved her. She worked hard, she took care of all the advertising, the catalogues, the special offers. She often came home late. I looked after your big sister. I had bought a record of nursery rhymes, it's a funny thing, I remember it perfectly, a record by Henri Dès from the Furet du Nord book and record shop, four euros ninety-nine centimes. I didn't know any of them. No one had ever sung nursery rhymes to me. I had grown up in silence, in a void, but I had survived and, despite everything, that was a mercy. But that's all over now. I'm tired.

Joséphine went to nursery. Your mother and I grew apart, we no longer behaved like twelve-year-olds, we had separate toothbrushes. All of a sudden we had grown older. And then, before you arrived, she thought maybe she didn't love me any more, and there would be no Mexico, none of the tenderness that follows love, that lasts to the very end; we were deeply saddened. I slept on the sofa. I drank wine in the dark. By the time I woke up with a sore head, your Mama had already gone to work and your sister was at nursery. I think it was then that I began to hate my life.

Twice As Much

I didn't know it. I felt it.

I felt wandering hands, greedy lips, longing eyes. I noticed new words that had insinuated themselves into our vocabulary. The pronounced way you'd tuck a strand of hair behind your ear. An unmistakable gesture. I felt a sense of evil. I felt the abyss. I felt my heart opening, tearing itself apart. I felt tears. I sensed the wild beast awakening. Anger growling. The storm, all the storms. I sensed the meaning of the word *sorrow*. The age-old sorrow of women. I tasted bitterness, dirt. I tasted fingers that smelled of lying. Betrayal. A glance slipping away. I would sit two millimetres further away from her. I tasted too much sugar in the coffee. I smelled the perfume of her new shampoo. Sweet almond soap. I was aware of shorter, more evasive, vaguer remarks. I was aware of her arm holding our little girl more tightly. Moist kisses. I was aware of unspoken apologies. Dolls that suddenly cost twice as much: small indulgences. I sensed fear. Breath coming shorter at night. Higher heels in the morning. Slightly redder lipstick. Longer fingernails. Claws. I was aware of a back. Bones. Pale skin. I sensed abandonment. Ecstasy. Brief moments of heaven. The odour of fucking. I felt the cold. The wind. The storm, all the storms. I felt my blood freezing. I felt cold water. I felt the world come crashing down. Nathalie had been unfaithful to me.

Fourteen Thousand Three Hundred And Eighty-One Euros

The burnt-out shell of the car was found by the police three days after it had been reported stolen, on the edge of a field in Wambrechies. It was a Renault Clio II, 2.0 16V, made in November 2006. The insurance company sent me to the scene to find out whether there was any possibility of fraud, going on the principle that the insured person was always presumed honest, so it was up to the company to provide proof, if there was any, that something was amiss. I had examined where the fire started (the front seat) and its progress (towards the bonnet). As this model did not have heated seats, I had immediately ruled out the idea that a short-circuit had caused the blaze. Experience showed that when a fire began in a car seat, it tended to spread along the back of the seat and reach the roof, which would begin to melt. The flames, fanned by the wind, would then lick the chassis, blistering and burning the paint, reaching a temperature of over a thousand degrees. I had inspected the Renault's anti-theft device and found no sign that the car had been broken into. Although the fire had destroyed 99 per cent of any potential evidence, I was still convinced that I was dealing with a fraud. So I went to see the owner of the vehicle, which she claimed had been stolen, and met a young woman who was six months pregnant. She asked me to sit down in her elegant little sitting room while she made two cups of coffee. There were no photographs on the mantelpiece or the chest of drawers. I asked her some questions about the circumstances of the theft; her replies seemed plausible, but it wasn't long before she burst into tears. It's only a car, I said, it isn't the end of the world, and it's not a rare model, a collector's item.

She shook her head. No, no, it's not that, she said. For a moment I thought about Nathalie and the way she sometimes cried when she was expecting Léon. She would put both hands on her swelling belly, look at me in tears, and I had no words to express our distress.

It's my husband, the young woman murmured. He's left me. He couldn't stand the idea of having a baby. I was the one who wanted it.

I put down my coffee cup.

So you threw out all the photos of you with him,

and you set fire to the car he had given you, and now you think your life is over?

She nodded, her tears preventing her from speaking. I remembered the day when Nathalie had come home from the hospital saying: that's it, it's over, gone, there's no baby now. I almost broke everything in our apartment, but instead it was inside myself that I allowed things to break – utopian dreams, clemency. That night I lay beside Joséphine, holding her in my arms, and her warm, regular breathing with its slightly sour smell of curdled milk lulled me to sleep. I had wanted to go back to the world of childhood that night, to its harmless illusions, blood that was only a colour and didn't mean pain. Nathalie had left the house, she slept somewhere else that night. No doubt she wanted to find words to explain it all, untrue words, acceptable shame.

I am paid to pay out as little as possible. I am paid to have no heart and no compassion. I have no right to reach out a hand to the shipwrecked sailor, there is no place in me for kindness. My capacity for pity has been eradicated, I have been turned into your average bastard, and I have let it all happen. I've had to say no to the misfortune of others. Isn't that so, Monsieur Grzeskowiak? I was required to let you sink, and in exchange you were left with the right to call me names. Obedience is the pride of cowards, our Legion of Honour.

All of a sudden the wild beast began to growl. It sank its teeth into my guts. I felt pain tapering to a point, and I let out a very long, shrill sound. The young woman jumped. But what if disobedience meant the beginning of peace? Disobeying, coming to a decision at the risk of endangering my life – just suppose there was salvation in that danger? A dignity that restored me to myself.

I am going to report that your car was indeed stolen, Madame, and that the thief or thieves then set fire to it, first dousing the driver's seat with combustible liquid, probably white spirit or de-icer, then spraying the same substance over the right-hand door and then the bonnet and that, given the presence of oxygen and some means of ignition, very likely a cigarette, the car then went up in flames.

Amid the mask of her tears, her sad smile became beautiful.

Why are you doing this?

I hesitated for a second.

To remind myself that I still have a heart.

Two days after I sent in my report, giving my expert opinion and agreeing to compensation at the current value of the car, namely fourteen thousand three hundred and eighty-one euros, I was summoned to company HQ.

I was fired.

Forty-Nine Francs Per Person

Several days before our first Christmas without them, we got a postcard from our mother showing the Eiffel Tower at sunset. Her handwriting was shaky. *I'm all right, I think of you three every day* (besides Anna and me, did she mean Anne or our father?) *Your mother who loves you. Happy Christmas.*

She had drawn a little star and two snowflakes – well, little circles, but my sister interpreted them as snowflakes. And that was it. Anna and I wept for the words she hadn't written. Words such as 'See you soon', 'We'll be together again, that's a promise', 'I'm so sorry', or 'I get scared without you.' I missed everything about her, even the kisses she hadn't given us when she was still here, everything she didn't do. Our father told us he had a nice surprise for Christmas Day. The nice surprise was the person with the silk blouse and the pretty breasts. He introduced her to us as a friend who was also alone on this happy day, adding that Christmas was a time when no one should be alone. *Mama today*, asked Anna. I translated. Is Mama alone today? I don't know, darling, I expect not, I expect she's with friends, people she knows from work, maybe. Our father had ordered the special Christmas Wonderland lunch from the Montois bakery, at forty-nine francs per person, with foie gras and beef tongue terrine, turkey breast, potatoes with chestnuts, and iced Yule log. There was ice throughout the meal. The guest who was going to be our father's wife gave us presents, but we refused to open them. She left the living room in tears. Then our father had slumped down in his seat and buried his face in his hands. I miss her too, he said. I rose to my feet to give one of the presents an almighty kick before taking refuge in my bedroom. We could have all gone to Bagnolet. To surprise her, to tell her that we needed her, to give her the latest novel by Sagan, *The Painted Lady*. We could have taken her a Wonderland lunch. Christmas wreaths. A little fir tree. Then we could have made her laugh so that she wanted to come back to us, to stop being sad, to switch off her sorrow. We could have helped her, Papa; we could have gone to find her, and save her. But that would have required so much love.

Eighty Euros (Continued)

My God, you wouldn't believe it. How do they do it? They sense everything, they know everything. And I can assure you I'm careful. Nothing in my diary, nothing on my mobile, a mobile is downright criminal, you think of it as an old friend, you think it'll keep all your secrets but that's utter crap. A mobile phone is a traitor. So no messages, no texting, none of that. I didn't tell a single soul but you, Antoine. But, believe it or not, she found out. I don't know whether she followed me or hired a detective or what, but anyway, she knew. I thought I was going to drop dead of a heart attack. It was six weeks ago, exactly the same date that you found out about your father. I went home after we'd had that drink, and there she was, reading in the living room, she's loved reading ever since she was a girl. Personally, I find books depressing. They're dry little furrows of words. A book is like a Japanese garden: kilometre upon kilometre of boredom. So I kiss her, same as usual. She suggests I have a glass of something while she finishes her chapter, it's a book she really likes, she can't wait to find out how it will end. I get myself a beer. I wait. Seems to be a long chapter, because I have time to open another beer. Then she gets up, looking at me. And at this point I feel there's something strange going on. There's a look in her eyes that I'd forgotten, the look she used to give me early on, when we made love all the time, when the world could have been ending and we wouldn't have cared. That look, Antoine. She looked as if she was ravenous, on fire. It was exciting and a bit scary too. We've calmed down a bit as far as that sort of thing is concerned, Fabienne and me; it's more like affection these days, bordering on friendship. We make love with words now; our actions are lethargic, even petrified, and here she was, giving me that volcanic look of hers again. Then she smiled at me. Oh, you, she said, just like that. Oh, you. Oh, me, what? And she repeated, Oh, you. I can tell you this was getting to me, it was freaking me out. But then we ate dinner as usual, she told me about her day at school, little Duquesnoy who's going to have to repeat a year, the new memo about break times, notice of strike action. She was going round and round in circles. It was torture.

When we got to dessert, and when I say dessert it

was only a yoghurt, she came out with it, just like that, her eyes burning: I'd like to learn how to suck you off too. Like your tart did. Teach me, Frédéric, I'm sure I'll be good at it. I sat there like a bloody idiot. With a mouthful of yoghurt, dripping from the corners of my mouth like some old guy's slobber. I must have been the same colour as that bloody yoghurt. Luckily I don't have heart trouble. I spat out the Danone. So you don't have to swallow? she asked, smiling. I swear, Antoine, I didn't know where to look. She got up, she came over to me, she knelt down beside me. Well? How does your tart do it? Show me. Don't be afraid of words, she told me, don't be afraid of words. It's easy to tell me not to be frightened of words, when I had only words of love for her. Suck is a loving word, she said, so is swallowing. On the other hand eighty euros, those words are disgusting. Truly disgusting.

Three Times Seventy Pence

Everything began the summer that Thomas gave Anna a cotton-grass flower in the Botanic Gardens on the Lautaret Pass. They were both seven; they both spoke the same half-language. They never left each other's side. They would put the same things on their plates: broccoli, cucumber, lettuce, Granny Smiths, all of them green. They liked sunset over the peak of La Meije, fizzy lemonade, songs by the Compagnie Créole that the monitors would sing in the evening. They promised each other things that only the three of us could understand. When they looked at one another there was something bigger than us between them, Léon, bigger than all of us. That rare, immense thing: joy. He was an only child; he was going to be her only love. His father worked in the chemical factory at Pont-de-Claix near Grenoble; ours was a chemist working at Lapchin's pharmacy in Cambrai. His mother was a dressmaker who worked from home; our mother had left home and got lost. Every spring we told Thomas where our next summer camp would be, and he would join us. I saw them growing up, I saw their singular love story blooming. And there was always that fascinating joy between them. At Morzines, Sallanches. At Aix-les-Bains. Summer after summer, it seemed to me that they talked less and less, as if words weren't quick enough for all they had to say to each other. They learned patience, they had an eternity ahead of them, and they knew it. One summer, we celebrated what we thought was Thomas's voice breaking with ten francs' worth of Haribo and friendship bracelets. His first step into the world of men. But it was only the start of a throat infection.

In 1985 we went to England, to Barnstaple in Devon. We ate fish and chips for the first time; it cost two pounds. I drank my first pint of lager, which cost seventy pence, then my second, and my third. I had my first hangover, and Anna cried.

That was the summer that I met Patricia and fell in love. I began to smoke because she smoked, I forgot about beer because she hated beer, I stopped mocking short people because she was short. I lost myself to find myself in her. I tried speaking words of love and failed, miserably. Even back then. You're pretty. I would like to live with you. I mean, I'd like us to see each other again. Er. Once we're back in France. I. I. I like kissing you.

And so on. All the way to her skin, her belly, down to the soft hair below. A room at the Cedars Inn, our bodies trembling, our mouths dry, suddenly mute, our first caresses, the first time for both of us. All that disorderly affection, the pain that no one had mentioned to me, like a knife cutting, a tear like tearing fabric, a drop of blood, the warm sense of shame, then laughter, an embrace, the wish to disappear. Even back then.

That's all it was. And it was all that.

Later, there was my abrupt departure from adolescence, the *Café de la Gare*, the celeriac remoulade that should have choked me, the letter, eighty centimes for the stamp, my betrayal.

In that last summer of childhood beside the River Taw, Anna and Thomas exchanged their first kiss. They were ten years old. It was a real, loving kiss. And in order not to spoil the blessing it brought, they said only these words. He said: *I*. She said: *love*. He said: *you*. For them, these were all the words in the world.

Less Than A Hundred Euros

Your mother didn't come back home straightaway. She came by after work and spent an hour or two with Joséphine; she gave her a bath, her dinner, a bedtime story, a cuddle, and then she left. I need to see clearly, she said – the unsatisfactory reply of someone who doesn't know how to tell you that she doesn't love you any more, and perhaps is already in love with someone else. Sometimes she came back again in the middle of the night, or at dawn. Sometimes she didn't. She brought with her the aromas of darkness: stale sweat, alcohol, musty perfume, small miseries. It was a strange time in our lives; we were a married couple with a child, but we didn't live like a married couple with a child. We had no plans for the coming summer. Or for the coming weekend. Or even for the day after next. Our life was spelled out in indifferent Post-It notes on the fridge door.

The babysitter moved into the house, into Joséphine's room. In the evenings, she sat at the kitchen table revising for her exams. I shut myself in my bedroom, drinking wine, as if it could quench the thirst of the beast inside me. My nights were painful, dark and violent; my dawns were purple, glaucous, sickly. And that thing inside me, still silent, was born. It made its way into my fears. It began to consume my shame. It fascinated me. It was beginning to take control.

FFF was like a big brother to me. He made me stock up the fridge, buy flowers, see my wife, talk to her, try to patch things up.

One weekend, Nathalie came back because she missed Joséphine. She was suntanned, having spent several days near Nice on a photo-shoot for her next catalogue – it would feature a mountain bike costing less than a hundred euros on the cover. She seemed happy. I didn't want her to be happy, not like that, I didn't like her quick, cheerful remarks, her suggestive comments, the scent of the other man on her skin, the smell of his tobacco in her hair. Around that time I accompanied FFF to Paris for a meeting organised by the Eurofins laboratory group on food safety. It was during the lunch break that I saw her. I would never have thought myself capable of even *seeing* another woman; Nathalie's indecision had not exhausted my hopes just yet. I still dreamed of mending our family and our marriage; I dreamed of an end to my torment. But she was a revelation. She was beautiful, of course, but what made her so immensely beautiful to me was her sadness. I fell in love immediately. I wanted to take that sad face in my hands. I wanted her shattering melancholy beside me. On my shoulder. My stomach. I wanted her on me, like a second skin. I wanted her here. I wanted her there. At the bar of a hotel with an unpronounceable name in Mexico or some such place. I wanted crisp sheets, clean smells, reconciliation, a prick as hard as stone – a life. I wanted to get my laughter back, my joy, I wanted the sweetness of her arms, to taste the fear that keeps us alive, the fear of losing one another. I wanted to drown in the breathtaking beauty drawn from her sadness; I had only drawn a sense of shame from mine.

Suddenly I felt faint.

Are you unwell? she asked. Yes. Or rather no. No, it won't do, I thought. I want to take you far away from here. Immediately. I want you to teach me how to love you. I'd like to make you laugh. I've never asked anyone this, but I'd like to swim in a lagoon with you, in blue, clear water, to drink a Blood and Sand cocktail with you, even though I don't know what that is. But no, it won't do. It won't do. I'd like . . . I'd like to be important to you. That's what I'd like. To be important to you. But I didn't dare say any of that. I'd never dared. I'll be all right, thanks, I said. I think it's the heat. We could go outside for some fresh air, she said. We could have a coffee or a glass of cold water, the conference doesn't start again until two, we have time.

I watched my mother leave, Léon. I watched my father refuse to fight to keep her. I saw his hands dangling hopelessly by his sides. I saw the unhappiness we'd had to live with ever since, I saw the tears that Anna and I shed when we stood on the stairs and saw our father asleep in the kitchen, his head on his plate because he'd drunk too much beer. So I took one last look at the sublime sadness of that woman, her immense beauty, and I realised it was indeed the last time I would see her. Running away never gets you anywhere. I read the name on her press pass. A sailor's name from a Gainsbourg song. Tears stung my eyes as I told her: I'm fine, thank you. A friend is waiting for me, an old friend, I said. Another time, perhaps.

Another time.

Thirty-Two Thousand One Hundred And Fifty Euros

I had lost my job at the age of thirty-seven. By then I was divorced with two children. I had pension payments outstanding. I had been accused of falsifying a report. Suspected of taking a bribe. Collusion. Fraud. Scams. I was a swindler, a crook. I understood everything. I saw how cowardly people were, I saw the yellow teeth of those whom I had fed, the whores' tongues of those who had licked me. Remembrance doesn't mean forgiveness. Nor does affection. I had saved them hundreds of thousands of euros in the case of the runaway Honda Hornet, tens of thousands on the dancing whiplash victim, and many millions more over all those years when I had been an expert assessor – cold, suspicious and honest to a fault. I had been an utter bastard, a perfect bastard. I'd been valued for that, they'd given me a rise for it. The managing director's secretary would simper whenever I passed her. I'd been given bonuses.

Two years earlier, I'd been given a company car as a Christmas present, and a secretary. Do whatever you like, but make sure she's here on time on Monday, ha, ha, ha. You've made so much money for us from cars, Antoine, that we thought you'd like this one. A BMW 320si. Thirty-two thousand one hundred and fifty euros; my thirty pieces of silver. I had driven home fast, skidding on the bends, accelerating towards amber lights. I was aroused. When I arrived home, I called out to Nathalie: pack a suitcase, I'm taking you to Tuscany. My mother used to say it was the most beautiful place in the world. Joséphine is asleep, she replied. When a child is asleep, passion goes to sleep too. We didn't go. And she thought the car was ugly; the colour was ugly.

I had slaved away for over fifteen years and a single second of compassion had made me a pariah. I had chosen this job to balance things out, to find that resting point between two parties, as Thomas Aquinas put it, where they both think they have a good deal. I had believed in justice, courtesy, beauty. And the right to disobey. I had believed in a 'time when men were kind . . . But tigers came at night'. I had defended myself as I had never dared defend myself before. I had landed a blow on the walls of their stupidity just as I used to land blows on the walls of my childhood bedroom, because I never wanted to hit my father again. I had talked about the changing world. The fortune they'd made from five billion's worth of unclaimed life insurance. Five billion! Think of all the good that could have been done with that.

But the hyenas were foaming at the mouth, their curved claws were scratching at the table. One of these days they'd tear out their own hearts. A rule is a rule. We paid you so that we wouldn't have to pay out, and we must have paid you too much, since you've become so generous. It's easy to be charitable with other people's money, Monsieur. I made a cowardly suggestion; I said I was prepared to reimburse the fourteen thousand three hundred and eighty-one euros paid out as compensation for the Clio. The hyenas laughed. The wild beast growled inside me. It wanted to leap at them and rip out their throats. Too late, I heard them say, you shouldn't have fallen for the pregnant woman. Who knows, for the price of her car, you might have got a little something in return? There were visions of carnage in my mind's eye. Blood everywhere. Scraps of skin. It's said that hyenas laugh while they're marking their territory. You will now hand back the keys to the BMW and the papers, along with your computer, your mobile phone, and all your files. We will report what you've done to our competitors. HR will see that you get a small unemployment benefit. And that's it. If you don't accept, go hire a lawyer.

Expenses

In primary school, we were fascinated by the word. It was a bad word, but not so bad you got detention for it. During break we would make our hands into horns and shout: Your Papa's a cuckold, your Papa's a cuckold. The word made some children cry, and some children laugh. But it wasn't funny, it expressed a terrible, eternal grief. A piece of the world melting, like a chunk of ice, diminishing its beauty, the reason for its existence, banishing them for ever. It cut to the quick; your skin burned, and nothing could soothe it. It was the beginning of the end of yourself. I looked for explanations, of course I did. But in vain. I felt hideous, and so I became hideous. You fade, that's what happens when you're not the chosen one any more, you become uncivilised, you despise yourself, you let yourself go. You eat badly, you become dirty, you start to smell. You wait for an angel to come along, a guardian angel who will watch over you and save you. But angels never come. People never rise back up, that's what's so sad about them. They always fall, with more or less distinction; their arms reach out into the void of their dreams, their fingernails break. Life is one long fall.

I didn't say anything to FFF because I was so ashamed, or to my father because he would have been ashamed of me, or to Anna because she would have been ashamed of Nathalie. I simply mentioned that we were having a few difficulties. That we needed to take a break. It was perfectly normal after the birth of a baby, I was told. Give it time. Couples are always reinventing themselves.

What rubbish.

Later, when my mother asks me about that period of my life, when she hears my story, she will smile a disillusioned little smile, light her two millionth cigarette with her usual grace, she will cough, and choke softly as she says these words: I did warn you, my dear, love doesn't count for much in the grand scheme of what women want.

What Nathalie wanted was the desire the agency's artistic director felt for her. The man who took her to Nice, Le Touquet, Cabo de Gata in Spain, to photograph bicycles and sports shoes for their catalogue. They would spend hours together on the train. Evenings in hotels with sea views. They would drink fine wine on expenses, their fingers intertwined. Nights far away from me and from Joséphine, far away from our life. And at dawn, after the savageries of the night, a sense of dizziness, breakfast together, the tattoo on his chest, Japanese characters spelling out *fukihonpou* – untrammelled, free – that made her lose her head. He was some kind of artist, I was some kind of bore. He shouted, made demands, tore things to pieces, whereas I thought, weighed things up, gave recommendations. Nathalie had been unfaithful to me because she didn't like being with me. She wanted fitting-room cubicles, looks charged with electricity, moments that wouldn't last. She wanted first times and last times. Our marriage offered certainty, duration, while she dreamed only of fevers, poisons – in those dreams she was so like my mother. I had thought the birth of Joséphine might herald the birth of the kind of love that changed things. But children's arms are too small and weak for that. They can't even hold up their own shadows. And then the artist got bored. He got a new tattoo on his shoulder: *ippokiookami* – lone wolf. Your mother loved it, but another woman was already waiting patiently in the wings. Nathalie came back to us more often. Joséphine took her first steps and said her first words. We bought a camera and tried to be a family. Then there were other nights away, because of work. Trips to Paris, missed trains, rooms at the Terminus Nord. A new babysitter. More glasses of wine. The beast was waking up, and with it the desire to go out at night with a broken bottle or a stone, to strike the barman who was rude because you hadn't tipped him enough, the jerk; to strike the old woman who pushed in front of you at the grocer just because she was old, the stupid bitch; to crush the guy who had almost dislocated your shoulder when he bumped into you because he's a bloody idiot, the little so-and-so. You wanted to attack the world because you didn't like it any more, and it didn't like you.

I wanted to give voice to everything I'd left unsaid, and then I wanted to sleep. Finally, to sleep.

Three Hundred Euros

So then your mother returned, and you came into the world. That was a wonderful time. I've kept the photographs. They show Joséphine putting cuddly toys in your cot. Doing drawings for when you arrived. Playing with dolls, learning how to change nappies on a Barbie doll – the point of which was not entirely clear. Your Mama is in them too. She is beautiful and ready to burst, with you. I thought our happiness had returned, Léon, I thought that the blood and waters of your birth would wash away our sins and bind us to each other. One day I had asked my mother whether she loved me, and she had replied by asking what use love was. What use was it? You had just been born when she died, leaving a horrible smell and a registered letter. She had left Bagnolet without telling us. She was living in a tiny studio in Pantin, paying three hundred euros a month. The area was full of prostitutes and junkies, a dismal place.

She had been dead for several days before the hot weather gave her away. We went there with your Aunt Anna and Uncle Thomas. Anna's tears stifled all her words, and heaven knows she had few enough of those already. Thomas was shaking; I'd never seen him shake like that. My sister wanted to be the first to see her. *You Antoine, wouldn't you see ugly.* You understand, Antoine, she wouldn't want you to see her ugly. But your grandmother was beautiful, Léon, she had a pale complexion, she was tall and slim, with Venetian blonde hair and dark eyes, and when she lit a cigarette her forearm moved with the grace of Nureyev.

When Anna returned to the landing she said, *She*, Thomas said, *is*, Anna said, *beautiful*, and I went in. That smell – you can't imagine it. The stench obliterated everything that was beautiful, seeping into your flesh, never to disappear.

I pray that we will be found quickly.

My mother was sitting in her bed, her back against the wall, her neck drooping, her head resting on her shoulder. The sheets were dark, dry and hard; sheets of meat. Her expression was fixed, her lips, lips that used to blow such pretty rings of mentholated smoke, had tried to say one last word, one petrified syllable. I stayed alone with her, with her body, and once again I didn't dare, Léon. I didn't dare to take her hand, or take her in my arms, I didn't dare to speak, to say my last words. I didn't dare to touch her or get close to her. I didn't dare make a sound or say her name. My tears were not for her death but for my cowardice, my fear, I was shedding tears for everything that she had never taught me and which, out of weakness, I hadn't ventured to learn.

My mother had left me in pieces so that I would grow up to be a man, she had abandoned me so that I would find myself; she had loved me in her own way, in her detachment, and I hadn't known it.

That's the love we lack, Léon. Motherly love.

Five Francs

The doctor diagnosed a catastrophic cerebrovascular stroke. Like a grenade going off in her head. But if it hadn't been that, it could well have been something else, he explained, acute respiratory disease, chronic obstructive pulmonary trouble, your mother was in very poor health.

The last time I had seen her alive I was thirty – two years before the grenade went off. She was still living in Bagnolet. The entrance to the tower block was squalid with graffiti, the smell of joints and the stale odour of shit. It was a small one-bedroom apartment and the smell of tobacco was overwhelming. I had knocked on the door, she had called out that it wasn't locked, and I had gone in. Her hair had turned white, and so had her skin. There were dark circles under her eyes which would have given her the 'smoky eyes' look if she'd been twenty, if she'd stayed with us, if she'd been happy. She didn't recognise me. What do you want? It's me, Mama, Antoine. Then she'd raised her exhausted eyes and smiled faintly: you should have warned me, my dear, I'd have made an effort.

I did warn you, Mama, I sent about fifty letters, a hundred letters, I wrote every year asking if I could come and see you, telling you it was hard for me and Anna to live without you, telling you it felt cold; I wrote asking you to come back and live with us. And you never replied, not even when I sent you a stamped, addressed envelope. Your silence screamed that you wanted to have nothing more to do with us.

But I didn't say any of that. I'm a coward and the son of a coward. Would you rather, I asked, I came back later?

Oh well, seeing you're here, sit down. Wait a moment, get me a beer, there's some in the fridge, and tell me what you're up to these days.

I talked to her for a long time. About growing up without her, without Anne, going to summer camp, Anna and Thomas, our father's remarriage. His wife in your bed, her jars of face cream on your side of the bathroom sink. The horrible presents she gave us when we were little. My cowardice with Frédéric Froment. My humiliations with girls. And Nathalie, the first time I'd ever felt love at first sight.

I didn't stop talking when her head dropped to her shoulder. And as she slept I talked about Joséphine's birth, my job, the lives I had ruined. Your absence, Mama, the menthol perfume I'd asked Papa to make so I could sniff it every evening before I went to bed, because it reminded me of your pretty hands. They never touched me, but I loved them. Finally I stopped talking. She was breathing heavily, her sleep was disturbed. Ghosts love misery, you see. There were beer cans on the table, an old newspaper, several worn books by her beloved Françoise Sagan. There were damp patches on the wall; one was shaped like the head of a small boar. A case of pareidolia, like seeing the man in the Moon. She had made the damp patches into a map of Italian cities; she'd marked Florence, Prato, Siena, Pisa, Arezzo, places she now went to on her own, without a suitcase, without a passport, without us, without anything. There was a little TV set on the floor, connected to the aerial of the apartment building next door. The kitchenette contained gas rings and canned food. I felt like weeping, like being a son at last, putting my arms around her and taking her away from this place, to the boar's head that looked like Tuscany, giving her one last chance to see beauty. Not filth and fear.

I stood up and went into the bedroom. There was a large mattress on the floor, medication, an empty bottle of water. And there, level with the bed, two photographs pinned near the skirting board. The first was taken in a five-franc photo booth, with a folded curtain as a backdrop. I was about six, my hair neatly combed, a white shirt buttoned up to the neck. My mother and I had taken that photo for the judo club. I had been happy that day. She had told me that I was handsome, and that I'd have a good life. All the women would fall in love with me, she said, and if I got things right – not too much poetry, Antoine, but a bit of muscle and plenty of nerve – I'd be a king among men. After the photo came out, she'd said: My word, you do look like a little man, and she'd planted a kiss on the black-and-white portrait. Then she had smuggled me into the Palace cinema. She bought ice-cream cones and we watched *That Most Important Thing: Love*. She wept over the beauty of Romy Schneider, and I was terrified by Claude Dauphin. I lay down on the floor in front of us so that I didn't have to watch, and she held my hand all through the film. That day, I was the happiest little boy in the world.

The second photograph showed the twins in the garden of our house. They were three or four years old, wearing pale pink dresses. They looked like sweets.

My mother began to cough, and I hurried over.

What were you saying, Antoine?

Rounded Down To Seven Hundred

That weekend you were both with me. It was the long bank holiday at the beginning of May. Nathalie had been back with the artistic director for two months. He had just added *ecchiwosuru* – screwing – to the collection of tattoos that chronicled his little life. She and I talked for a long time. We drank wine. We shed tears. We held each other close. We felt frightened and cold. We remembered the birth of Joséphine, her perfect little nails, her long lashes, her strawberry mouth. The terrible months that followed. The abortion. Nights on the sofa. The smell of other men. Then our reconciliation and finally your arrival, Léon.

We shed tears for our failed life. For having burned our bridges. I tried not to mention the shame I felt; *on the dole, unemployed*. She tried to apologise, but I didn't want to hear apologies. She kissed me on the lips one last time. It was a long, forceful, feverish kiss. I whispered one last time that I loved her, she blushed, and then she left. Later, you children would join her, when the artistic director remembered that she had two children and agreed to make some room for them.

Until then I would do my best; I would be the opposite of my father.

I learned to use the washing machine, taking care to wash whites and colours separately. I learned to use bleach to get rid of limescale. Black Briochin soap to clean the oven. I'd put a drop of oil in the water when boiling pasta so it wouldn't stick. I learned answers to the questions you and your sister would ask me some day. (Why does it rain, Papa? Why is a year in the life of a dog like seven human years? Why don't you go to work any more?) I learned to say I loved you when you showed me a drawing, a neatly tied shoelace, a tidy bedroom.

I tried to give you what I had never had.

That weekend something happened. The kind of thing that always happens on public holidays – a radiator in the house began to leak. Then water started pouring out. You shouted: Papa, Papa, there's a pond in the living room! I had learned the name of the planet furthest from Earth (Neptune) and the name of the planet closest to Earth (Venus), but I hadn't learned how to fix a leak. Joséphine proudly produced one of the thousands of flyers that regularly came through our letterbox. *The Lads for Your Leaks*. I called the number. Sure, fine, no problem, be with you in fifteen minutes. Do you remember how you reacted when the plumber arrived? You flinched. He looked like a sumo wrestler. His puffy, sunken eyes located the leak. Then he took some kind of key out of his pocket, did battle for twenty seconds, and the water stopped. Then he wanted to check all the other radiators in the house. The same could happen to any of them. Then he wanted to check the flushing mechanism in the toilet. The danger was everywhere. The water flowing into the kitchen, into the bathroom. Ah, he said. I needed an O-ring and I didn't have one. An O-ring? Without it, you'll be calling me back in three hours' time, your bathroom will be a swimming pool. Oh. Yes, there's too much pressure after the radiator episode. *The radiator episode*, fancy that. So what's to be done? I tell you what, I'll call a mate, he'll help me out. The sumo wrestler sat down on one of the dining-room chairs, and your sister stifled a cry. Luckily the chair withstood his weight. He took a piece of paper and a pencil from out of his bottomless pocket, and wrote down the first figure: eighty euros. Then: a call-out on a public holiday, that's a supplement of thirty-five euros; bleeding a radiator thirty euros, thirty euros times eight equals two hundred and forty euros; repair of faulty radiator joint fifty-three fifty; labour – I arrived at ten to eleven, it's eleven-thirty now, I'll only charge you for half an hour, that'll be seventy-five euros plus the public holiday supplement, fifty per cent, call it thirty-seven fifty. I was about to say something like *stop messing me around* when the doorbell rang. A smile crossed the plumber's curious lips. It'll be the O-joint, an O-joint's not that expensive, ninety-three centimes; calling out my mate eight euros, I won't charge you the installation fee or the public holiday supplement for him; plus VAT, in all, plus this, take away that, there we are, seven hundred and nineteen euros eighty-nine, I'll round it down to seven hundred for you. I was going to protest, but he was already on his feet and heading towards the front door to let his colleague in. Another mound of flesh.

I got the idea. I'd been well and truly fucked, as FFF would say. He'd fucked me over just like the queue-jumping old lady, the taxi driver who takes the long way round, the cop who fines you thirty-five euros for honking your horn behind a double-parked 4×4, because your horn, Monsieur, is to be used only in situations of immediate danger, see paragraph R416-1 of the Highway Code. But that guy in front is allowed to park there holding up everyone else? Your ID, Monsieur, get out of your vehicle.

All these irritations, humiliations, all that shame. Years of bruises, a whole childhood of bruises and repressed anger.

And then one day you see it in the way your kids look at you; there's such an unspeakable distance between you already. Their polite, cautious contempt; you're no hero, that's for sure, you'll never be one. Why did you pay them, Papa? Joséphine asked once the two monsters had left. They're just dirty thieves, we ought to call the police. The police. The guardians of the peace. Lost dreams. And you added: Dirty thieves, I'd smash their faces in.

It was the straw that broke the camel's back.

That, Léon, was the day the tiger awoke, and it never went back to sleep.

Three Hundred And Ninety-Nine Euros
Ninety-Nine

The size 52 fitted him like a glove. He had lost even more weight, but seemed to have settled at that size. It was a good suit, dark blue Prince of Wales check, and it cost three hundred and ninety-nine euros ninety-nine centimes. He had regained the elegant figure he had in the black-and-white photos of his wedding to our mother one chilly day in January about a thousand years before, before we even existed, when anything seemed possible and their love would only add lustre to their lives. But then I came along and shattered their dreams.

I had been the beginning and the end.

We don't know it's just a question of waiting now the doctor says there's nothing more we can do and after all he's the one who has the final say he's the one well when I say he's the one it's that he has the last word you see your father could still be here tomorrow or in a month's time or in six months' time six years' time or he could go right now we don't know we don't know any more and when I ask him what would be best for him what he'd like to do before I mean before this horrible thing happens he looks at me with a smile not a nasty smile but not a really nice smile either no I think it's a sad smile it's melancholy when life isn't what you want any more he won't reply to me I really wish he'd tell me what he'd like to do but maybe he wants me to go away only he doesn't like to say so it's hard to tell someone you don't need them any more it's very hard it's a terrible torment the bitterness of not having loved what you're leaving enough.

Enough To Pay The Rent

We stayed for several days in Bagnolet, Anna, Thomas and I. We asked the neighbours questions.

A nice woman. Quiet. She lived with a guy for a few months, he was younger than her. Then another guy, but he didn't sleep there, maybe he had a family. He sometimes shouted. But no one complained. If you complain around here your mailbox gets burnt, you get shit on your doormat, your cat turns up dead.

I liked her, she must have been very beautiful once. I was always telling her she smoked too much. She introduced me to that Sagan woman. Her books are good, I like them a lot.

She used to work at the supermarket on Avenue Gambetta. She left at four or five in the morning to clean the shop, she was afraid of the big machine that did the floors so she washed them by hand with a mop. She said she used to have pretty hands in the old days.

She was a brave woman. No, she never talked about her former life. I didn't even know that she had children. But you could see that she'd suffered. She never complained. In the afternoon she used to clean for Dr Humbert near the Parc Jean-Moulin. The family was good to her. She liked going there. It was the Humberts who gave her that little TV. She loved watching it. She used to say she missed Léon Zitrone, he was better-looking and had better diction than most of the presenters today. She left when they fired her from the supermarket. They fired everyone so they could hire younger people who'd cost less, they're scum if you ask me. She didn't even have enough money left to pay the rent. Sorry, I don't know where she's gone, I haven't heard from her.

You mean she was your Mama? And you never came to find her?

Three Euros Ninety-Five, Four Eighty

Anna and Thomas were worried because I couldn't find another job. I had several interviews, but nothing came of them. My CV landed in the bin along with the three and a half million other candidates who'd been rejected. Anna invited me to dinner often: You mustn't be on your own, silence is bad for you, she said, it whispers sad things in your ear. They had been happy together since they were seven; for twenty-five years. They were beautiful. After they turned sixteen they were constantly together. Thomas came to Cambrai to live with us. He made us happy, the storm clouds dispersed, and sometimes our father even smiled. We had finally made an effort to accept his wife. We no longer mourned our mother's absence. We had become adults, which was another form of cruelty.

And then I left our house to live with Nathalie. My great love story. Thomas and Anna had decided, early on, not to have children and when our father's wife asked them one evening why not, they said some sorrows ought to end with them. After their Baccalaureat, they studied literature at Lille 3 University. Then they began to write books – together. Like Delly. Like Nicci French. Stories with happy endings. Not like real life.

Write a book, Thomas suggested to me one day, smiling. It might help. Oh, I'd never be able to. Don't think like that, Antoine; Cioran said that a writer writes about his shame.

Nathalie was furious because I could no longer pay her much maintenance. She wanted me to sell our house, she wanted more than half the proceeds. You and Joséphine didn't come to see me so often. The artistic director had become your hero. He was tattooed. Exotic. His name was Olivier, like a southern tree. He went to the seaside to photograph sandals, and to the mountains to photograph backpacks. FFF looked for cheaper offices for us. You must have an office, he said, a telephone, your name on a door. You must stay among the noise of the world or the very idea of unemployment will consume your prostate and screw your colon. Stay in the thick of it, Antoine, anger will keep you afloat.

We no longer hung out together in the evenings, drinking beer. He went home early. He never went on one of his sole missions again; Fabienne had taken charge, and he no longer strayed into the mouths of little tarts. Go and see her, Antoine, why don't you, it would relax you, you look uptight, repressed, you look like you've a poker up your arse with your sad tale of woe, your creased shirt, your rubbish trainers. Grief isn't attractive, you know. While you're waiting to find a nice girl and start thinking about putting your life together, getting your kids' respect back, why don't you go and visit that tart and get her to see to you.

But I didn't dare. I never dared.

I always went straight home. I heated up a Picard ready meal for one, paella Valenciana for three euros ninety-five, chicken korma and basmati rice, three eighty. My hands shook. I wasn't the man I used to be. Sometimes I wept because once upon a time I was a good guy – or so I thought – doing an honest job, part of a family that I had tried to save. I had tried my hand at forgiveness but my cowardice got in the way. I had tried to find my mother, but she didn't want to be found, she had preferred the violence of solitude to the absence of passion, accepting that she would fall because she had never managed to climb high enough. She had let herself live, but she would rather have died of love.

A love story could be short, she had said, but it had to be so intense you could die, you *must* die at the end.

Nothing but that kind of love will do, my little boy. But that which is wanting cannot be numbered.[*]

I had internalised my father's hatred. I had given him a chance, he had taken it; he had smiled and reminisced. Had regretted what we could have been. His illness was gnawing away at him, but he had wanted to take me back to the time of Patricia, the good times. In his own way, he was asking me to forgive him. I had put my arms round him that evening, and held him close, the way a father holds a child who has fallen and can't get up. I shed tears, I muttered the unthinkable: I've missed you so much, Papa, so very much. My father's wife sobbed and hid in their bedroom. We were on our own, my father and I. He rubbed his reddened eyes. Hyphema, a pooling of blood in the eyes. He was an old dog.

Sometimes I want to die too, Papa.

[*] Ecclesiasticus, 1.15.

One Thousand

Made by the Yanks. The inventors of the Western. Of Smith and Wesson. Stinger missiles. The Hummer. Dirty Harry. It's sound, mate. Top quality. You can hit your man between the eyes from five metres. One metre and you'll nuke him. His skull will be meat. 0.22 calibre. Five rounds. Not much recoil. A really mint gun. The chicks love it. Easy to hide in a bag. I've just been reassembling one. Only fired once, in Marseille. No trace, no number. Unspoiled goods, man. Well, show us the cash, then. I've got other deals to do. One thousand, right.

I dared, for the second time in my life. I dared to cross the motorway and venture into the underbelly of south Lille. I entered the city's intestines; its long, creepy tunnels. I was jostled, accosted, threatened; I was on a ghost train at the world's most awful fairground. Did I want dope, girls, phones? Or did I want a gun? A gun, I muttered. I was terrified. I was ready to shit myself. I'd empty my bowels where I stood then melt into the filth.

It'll cost you a thousand. Tomorrow, *la noche*, the Parc de l'Aventure. We'll find you. If you don't turn up, we'll find you.

When I got home, I was sick. I couldn't sleep. I imagined them coming to rob me, bleed me to death. Or catch me. They could be undercover cops. I was one of life's victims, as well I knew. I'd been told so. I'd already received that wound and I expect that was why I went back the following day, to the edge of the precipice, with a thousand euros in my pocket. Because of all the humiliations and the wounds.

You see, I am finally capable of doing something I would never have dared do before. I don't have to cross at the pedestrian crossing if I don't want to. I can give a bastard the finger. I can talk shit. To anyone I want. I can tell anyone to fuck off. Fuck off, Nathalie. And you, you tattooed bastard, fuck off. Go fuck yourself. It's *kusoku-rae* in Japanese – you see, I know some stuff, too. The whole damn lot of you can go fuck yourselves. My anger is drowning me, it scares me. I'm drunk on it.

The shadowy fingers took less than twelve seconds to count my twenty fifty-euro notes. By the time they got to the thirteenth, there was a Ruger LCR-22 in my pocket.

Six Months' Pay

I went back to see my father. He was looking good in his Prince of Wales check suit; one last handsome photograph. His eyes watered.

His eyes are always watering these days I don't know if it's the medication or some kind of deep-set grief maybe it's for me because I'm alive because he's going to lose me do you think his smile will come back?

I reassured them both; I lied like a good son. Yes, I'm looking for a new job, there are some interesting opportunities. I'm going to interviews. I may be appointed to a committee investigating MOT test fraud.

You're so talented Antoine that's what your Papa is always telling me but it's sad all the same that you were fired it must have been a shock a cousin of mine was fired from Vallourec he never got over it he left with six months' salary but it only lasted him three months and then it was gone.

They were at what I like to think of as the 'pyjama' stage of their lives, and I found that moving. Their movements were restricted. They had a quiet kindliness; they didn't want to put anyone out. My father had been happy in modest, limited circumstances; he had never spread his wings, had never raced down a pontoon to catch a boat. He'd taken my mother's hand and immediately dropped it because it scalded him. He had turned his back on his love of poetry, on his dreams of science and winning a Nobel Prize. He had continued to work for the Lapchin pharmacy, making up thousands of prescriptions, donning his white coat every day. As far as he was concerned, clothes made the man, and his white coat fitted perfectly.

The three of us watched *Singin' in the Rain*, and when the film was over I hugged my father and kissed his hands. At the door his wife thanked me: you're a good son, it's good what you're doing for him.

I smiled at her. You're a lovely person, Colette.

She stifled a sob. That's the first time in thirty years you've called me by my first name.

I had dinner one last time with Anna and Thomas. When I left, Anna whispered something to me. *Choose the day*.

Choose the day. But then night consumed me.

All The Gold In The World

In the end it wasn't such a bad idea that your mother decided to go to Leucate to take photos for her spring catalogue. That gave us a week together, just for us, and we were able to catch up with one another. You've noticed how your sister is beginning to be funny. Yesterday, she mimicked my father's wife, she started talking the way she talks, like a machine gun, never stopping, never taking a breath until I thought she was about to faint and fall to the ground. It was brilliant. You're more secretive, Léon, you look at your shoes, you don't use so many words, you're like me, you keep yourself to yourself. One day, that will become a burden, a burden that is too heavy to bear. I hope you've been happy. We had a lovely day today, the best day of all, of our whole life together, even better than the day you were born. You can't have regrets after a day like that. Did you know that the Othello, that chocolate meringue they serve at the Montois bakery, used to be called a Negro's Head? They changed its name because of the word *negro*. Because of what it's OK to say or not to say. But people can still be treated like dirt, fired on the spot, dumped for no good reason. Left to suffer alone. That's the way of the world. That's our place in the world. You're not allowed to complain. It doesn't make for a good life. Well, that's all over now. Sometimes there is no point in carrying on. It's all very well for people to tell you that you have to fight, but it's bullshit. You can have all the money in the world and it's still bullshit. Look at my father and that fucking cancer of his. He's not going to win that fight. It's hungry, it's going to eat him alive. He's going to die in a filthy way. We have to know when to stop, Léon. That's one gift we are given: knowing when the end has come. Take your bow. Give them the finger. Tell them: you're not going to hurt me any more.

Today we're going to put an end to this, Léon. Your sister has just gone. I cried when I put the pillow over her head. She's so pretty. My hands were shaking. I barely touched the trigger. The recoil surprised me. I know she didn't suffer. You don't suffer, it happens so quickly. So very quickly. I'm not sad. No one can be sad when the end to their suffering is in sight. It's just like my little sister Anne, the one who never woke up. This is my goodbye. I'm telling you that I love you. And that if there are days when it rains, that's because Tane separated his parents. He pushed Papa with his arms and Rangi with his feet until they were driven apart. Ranginui became the Father Sky. Papatuanuku became the Mother Earth.

The rain, Léon, it's my immense grief.

And Joséphine cried out: Papa, Papa, I'm covered in blood, my mouth hurts.

The desire to kill, or to destroy oneself and everything around one, always goes hand in hand with a great desire to love and be loved, a great desire to merge with the object of your love and thus for its salvation.[*]

* Louis Althusser, *The Future Lasts Forever.*

Part Two

1922

The hotel is called Desconocido. It is on the west coast of Mexico, sixty miles south of the city of Puerto Vallarta, in the heart of a nature reserve. The stilts its *palofitos* are built on are graceful; they dip into the Pacific Ocean like a woman testing the bathwater with her foot. There is a bar where they serve Blood and Sand, a cocktail created in 1922 for the film of the same name, starring Rudolph Valentino. It's the story of a matador. Violent passion. Blood and Sand. Twenty millilitres of whisky, twenty of cherry liqueur, twenty of red vermouth, twenty of fresh orange juice. With a twist of citrus peel for decoration. I have just ordered my second. The blades of the fan turn gently above my head, like calm and regular breathing. The Norwegian couple are sitting in their usual place. They drink champagne in silence. Soon the Indian and his daughter will come to eat fish from the day's catch and vegetables brought up from the village. There are no windows, only large openings. The temperature is not so fierce now. The sun looks like a large orange, its reflection in my glass like fire. Soon it will sink into the sea and night will fall. The beast has gone. Night holds no terror for me now. I have been here for nearly four weeks. The money that I brought with me has fed me. Washed me. Helped me to put on a little weight. I have said very little. My schoolboy Spanish has slowly resurfaced and with each passing day I manage longer sentences. My mistakes make people laugh. They offer me more words, like crutches. They would dearly like me to be able to make myself understood. Here, a man who expresses himself poorly is an animal. A *pendejo*. I have learnt to sleep again at night. I have spent hours walking along the beach, just a step away from the murderous appetite of the ocean, and it hasn't caught me. I let those I loved go. My father's eyes were still watering when I left them all. They were alive. We should not be alive.

No one knows me here. I have no past. I have never held a Ruger. Never pulled a trigger. I come from Europe, from France. Ah, Paris, Paris! I am still a little too thin. My skin has darkened under the sun. My hair is beginning to go white at the temples. The green that my mother loved shines again in my eyes.

Desconocido. Unknown.

Her cry woke Léon. He cried out too, when he saw his sister's face covered in blood. When he saw the gun in my hand. The pillow in my other hand. I rushed towards Joséphine. The bullet had gone through her jaw, exposing the bone. My daughter collapsed in my arms. Dial 15, Léon. Call the number 15. Quick. Say it's a gunshot wound. To the face. A child. Hurry. Hurry.

Six minutes later, our lives were annihilated.

The police arrived. I was separated from my children. The police tried to contact Nathalie, but couldn't. Then they called my father's wife. They sent a car for her. They brought in more doctors. Some of the police officers sent curious neighbours home. Paramedics had already taken Joséphine to the University Hospital.

In the kitchen, where I had been shut in, the police officer on guard eyed me with disgust. Then with infinite sadness. Trying to do something like that to your own kids. Bloody hell. He told me to give him my shoe-laces and my watch. And to empty my pockets.

My father's wife arrived. Léon ran to her. It's over now all over I'm here Léon we'll go back to my place your grandpa is expecting you he's made hot chocolate we're going back to my place you can have a bath and rest or if you like we'll watch a film we've got lots of nice films musicals oh my God what happened whatever happened here it's not as if we don't have enough unhap-piness this was all we needed ... A woman gently placed a hand on her shoulder to make her stop. Then they left the house, Léon walking between them in his soiled pyjamas. A small, shattered doll. And then there was the void. The abyss.

I was not handcuffed but I was pushed firmly towards a car. I fell into it. My guard sat down beside me. His eyes never left me, nor did his hatred dimin-ish. We set off. The flashing light was put on but no siren. This was more of a curiosity than front-page news: man shoots eleven-year-old daughter. Nothing to rouse the whole neighbourhood for. At the police station the duty sergeant recognised me and gave me a sad smile. I told you, he said, the dustbin of human misfortune, Monsieur. Go into this room, someone will be along shortly. I asked for news of my daughter. Someone will be along shortly, Monsieur. Is she?

Someone will be along shortly, Monsieur. No one came.

At dawn I was taken to the secure ward of Lille University Hospital in an ambulance. I was fastened to a bed. I had needles stuck in my arms. I lost consciousness several times. The warmth of my piss comforted me, the stink of my shit. I refused to eat. I wanted to die. They stuck another needle in me. I was no longer hungry or thirsty. I tried to swallow my tongue and brought up bile. Nurses came and went, looking after me. They were kind.

Is my daughter?

We don't know, Monsieur. We don't even know if she's in this hospital.

Then, much later, someone did come, with a smile.

60

I am alone. I came here alone.

After more than three years spent with doctors, being brainwashed by medication, I found that female journalist again, the one who bore the name of a great admiral in the British navy and of a Gainsbourg album.

She didn't remember me. I don't know what you mean, she said. I don't know what you're after. Anyway, I'm with someone. I'm married. I talked about her sadness, her infinite beauty. A blue lagoon. A cocktail named after a film, a twist of orange peel on the rim of the glass. I talked to make her laugh. I talked about a life, I talked about her. The improbable lifeline that had kept me from drowning, had kept me afloat on a sea of misfortune; all those long months spent in a blank void, in the ether, surrounded by metallic sounds, as the rest of the world lay silent. Three years of chemicals and restraints. She said nothing, but hung up the phone.

Both parties must be wounded, both must be searching, if one is not to crush the other with fatal results. I held the receiver in my hand for a long time, against my ear. A small plastic pistol. I let my last dream fade away.

The house was sold. Nathalie got more than half of the proceeds and I used the rest to get me here. Here, where I had dreamed of starting our lives anew. Of epic, tragic love stories, a love that would be brief but infinite. They shot *The Night of the Iguana* only a few miles from here.

There are twenty-seven *palafitos*. They are all named after cards in the Mexican lottery. I am in *el valiente*. The brave man. Fate can be cruel. It is my last night in this incredible place, this little house that dances, like a saucer bug, on an island between water and sky. Yesterday morning, one of the cleaning ladies didn't turn up on the van that brings them every day from El Tuito, the neighbouring village on the outskirts of the reserve. The silence of the other five suggested some misfortune. Tigers roam by night. I don't know what came over me, but I asked if I could take her place. Please; my mother was a cleaner, I know what's involved. I'm not worried about ruining my hands. They are strong and solid, like my mother's. I can't go on paying seven thousand seven hundred pesos a day. For this kind of work, Monsieur, you would be paid sixty pesos a day; if you worked for a year you'd be able to stay here for two nights. I don't think you realise. I said, Yes, I do realise. I said I would like to work here and earn sixty pesos a day. *El loco. El loco.* That day, I became known as the madman. But I had been silent ever since I arrived and that spoke in my favour. In my discretion I became inoffensive. The hotel staff felt compassion towards me. Later, my colleagues would tell me that they had assumed I was there because of some sad and hopeless love story – which was not entirely untrue. That I walked so close to the ocean because I wanted it to swallow me up. Like the *suicida* who had written *Under the Volcano*. People thought I might have come here to write a novel. Write the words in blood, like making mad love. They thought the magic of the Desconocido had saved me. So I became a cleaner. I rent a tiny room in El Tuito for ten pesos a day.

We set off at dawn every morning, seven days a week. Fifty minutes in an uncomfortable van along mud roads. A long, long cloud of dust in the air behind us. Sometimes I try to catch it; hold it. The women laugh. And words come through the bars that their fingers form over their mouths. *¡El loco! ¡El loco!* I laugh with them, and with every passing day my laughter becomes lighter; it becomes graceful even, free from the grief of the past.

One day, this laughter will take me to her.

Why did you never go looking for your mother?'

Although a sticker forbids it, he lets me smoke. I inhale until it burns my lips and tongue. Then I exhale. For a moment, the smoke stays in the air in front of my face, hiding it, like the apple hiding the face of Magritte's *Son of Man*.

'I was waiting for her to come back. I thought a child was so important that a mother would always come back. Apparently not. I kept wondering why she hadn't taken me and Anna with her. Why she had just left us with our father. We tried to go and see her once. The train was very expensive, hundreds of francs, and we didn't have that kind of money. I promised Anna I would find the money somehow, steal it if I had to. But I never dared. I don't know why, maybe I was afraid of being caught and punished. No. It wasn't that. I was afraid of something else – of discovering that she could live without us; that she could be happy without us. I was scared she might not be suffering; that she didn't need us. Like frogs, who abandon their tadpoles in a pond without a second thought. Or sea turtles, who bury their eggs in the sand, leaving their babies to hatch alone, reach the water alone, survive alone. Maybe she was a sea turtle. I didn't want to find out. I didn't want to see her holding someone else. I never dared ask my father whether she had any other children, or another family, a little girl perhaps. Whether I had a brother. She abandoned us to our father. I think that Anna and I grew up in her absence rather than in his presence. It was when my mother's neighbour asked the same question as you did – why had I never looked for my mother – that I understood. It was because she didn't love me. One day I had asked her whether she loved me and she answered, but what use is that? No child ought to hear a thing like that. It killed me. I mean, it was what began to kill me.'

I light another cigarette. He looks at me. His gaze is gentle. His smile is kind.

'So that began to kill you,' he said.

'The last time I visited her she was coughing a lot. It was the last time I saw her, ten years ago now. I told her what had become of us all, but she fell asleep as I was talking. I remember looking at her and thinking that this was the moment. That I should put my arms around her and take her home. But we no longer had a home. My father's wife had taken over. Nathalie and I were breaking up. Anna and Thomas were living in a studio. We no longer had a home because we no longer had a Mama, I think. When she left, on the day of the funeral, she took the idea of family and home with her. The desire to stick pictures on the fridge. She left only absence. My father with his head on his plate as my sister and I sat on the stairs. And that is why I didn't put my arms around her. Or take her away with me that day. I left her to her ashtrays, her beer cans and books. And I never saw her again. Do you know if my daughter

XVI

It was the Aztecs who called it El Tuito, in the sixteenth
century. Two translations have been suggested: The
Valley of the Gods, or The Place of Beauty.

There are yellow and orange houses made of local
mud and clay. Red tiles. Palm trees. A square, a colo-
nade, and in the middle of the square a huge tree
that the villagers have called Maria. The farmers who
live here also work for local hotels, including the
Desconocido. Vans and pick-up trucks deliver mangoes,
oranges, lemons and guavas every day. The livestock
farmers supply meat, but most people prefer fish. Blue
marlin, yellowfin tuna, red carp, swordfish. I have been
living here for two months now and I still don't know
whether I've begun to put myself back together again.

We set off at dawn for La Cruz de Loreto. We begin
work at the Desconocido, cleaning the wooden pon-
toons, and sometimes oiling them. Then the huge

palafito containing the bar, the restaurant, and the impressive billiard table. Then the villas, when the guests have raised a blue flag to show they are ready. They raise the red flag for breakfast, and the white when they need something else. There are no telephones in the rooms, no electricity or hot water. It's an eco-hotel, drawing on the natural resources of the reserve. Drinking water comes from an aquifer. Solar panels provide hot water and electricity in the kitchen. I felt disorientated at first, but it was wonderful to discover a life ruled by the sun and the colour of the sky. To spend evenings by candlelight in the middle of nowhere, with the deceptively peaceful sound of the ocean in the distance. I like cleaning. I have learned how to remove stains left by wax, lipstick and blood (without hot water). How to dislodge sand in the cracks between the floorboards. I am responsible for five *palafitos*, and I like the guests who occupy them, but when they have left, I also like to make them disappear – every hair, every last trace of perfume – so that the next occupants will feel that they are the first and think themselves in paradise. We leave in the late afternoon, when the beds have been made ready for the evening, the water tanks are full, and there are flowers on the bedside tables. Some days I stay a little longer to walk beside the ocean, and leave in the last delivery van. Then I go back to my tiny room, which is like a cell. For two pesos the manageress of the boarding house will make me tacos or *tostadas*, for another two she will give me a glass of *raicilla*, which burns my stomach and helps me fall asleep.

The nightmares have gone; I no longer wake in tears. I don't need tablets any more. I celebrated my fortieth birthday in silence. I am working as a cleaner in a hotel on the west coast of Mexico. My friends drive vans loaded with fruit and teach me how to bleach linen. We laugh together in the evenings, in the shade of Maria, the gigantic tree. And when they ask me to tell them about my life before I came here, I tell them for the tenth time that I am running away from a woman, an *exaltada*, an *hambrienta d'amor*, and they laugh more than ever, while my own laughter gently dies away. Then I have the feeling that I have found peace at last.

Maybe Three

For a long time, I had no news of her. I didn't know whether she was still alive or whether I had murdered my own daughter. Not knowing was the most painful part. No one would answer my questions. No one talked to me. I was floating in a void. I tried to drown myself under the shower, to choke myself by swallowing my own shit. To bite through the skin of my wrist, to open my veins and let the poison spurt out. It would be thick and sticky. Definitive. I was saved from myself every time. They wanted me alive. They wanted to understand, to perform an autopsy on the horror, explain it. I remembered photographs. Joséphine kissing her mother's belly. Joséphine drawing, painting, making all those presents to welcome her little brother. My daughter is beautiful. Anna wanted to visit me. They wouldn't let her. No one else asked to see me, not Nathalie, not FFF. Not my father's wife.

I was a monster. The polite, charming, smiling neighbour. A man without a past. He never said strange things or looked shifty. He tidied up after himself, you wouldn't even catch him stubbing out a cigarette on the pavement. But still, his wife left him. He was fired from his job for accepting a bribe, I think. His father is disabled or something. And his mother . . . His mother died in appalling conditions. He abandoned her.

I was a father who had injured his daughter and who was about to do the same to his little son. But for the shaking of my hand.

I had wanted to put an end to our cowardice, I had wanted my heritage to stop with me. But my hand was shaking when I went to shoot my daughter and the bullet had blown off part of her face.

I had wanted to make sure that no thoughtless person could ever hurt them, could ever destroy their lives. But my hand was shaking and I had failed even in that.

Gentleness. The end of things.

Our goodbyes had not been said.

Then one day, a year later, an eternity later: your daughter is alive. Joséphine is alive. I shed tears. Can I see her? Please. I begged. How is she?

The doctors were cold and factual. Like scalpels.

She can't smile yet. She will always have a slightly

deformed jaw. After several skin grafts, maybe three, the scar will almost disappear. She will need speech therapy to be able to speak properly again. With time and patience, there will be almost no sign of what happened to her. Surgeons can work wonders these days. Miracles, even.

But what miracle can they work to make sure that, one day, Joséphine will have a good life?

¡El loco! ¡El loco! I turned round. The boy was about ten years old. I immediately thought of Léon. As I remembered him. Leon had been a little taller, just as thin, but also a little younger.

He had been eight when I last saw him, on that night almost five years ago. He had left without a parting glance, walking between my father's wife and another woman in his soiled pyjamas, miserable and afraid. He hadn't come to see me in hospital when they decided, a year later, that I was not dangerous. He hadn't wanted me to visit him when I came out, on the eve of his twelfth birthday. I had written him a letter, but I don't know whether he ever read it, or whether Nathalie even gave it to him. It will take time, I was told. Re-establishing contact will be a slow and painful business. It will most likely never happen. Don't set your heart on it, for the moment. Set yourself another goal.

Don't stop trying – by standing still, you'll fall.

The child was holding a football under his arm. An old piece of patched leather that had been mended several times. I had noticed him before; he was always on his own. The T-shirt he wore was too big for him. He'd dribble the ball round the colonnade in the square and try to score goals against the trunks of the palm trees. He was touchingly clumsy, disarmingly stubborn.

¡El loco! ¡El loco! I turned round again. He looked at me; his eyes were very dark. Then he showed me his smile; his last milk teeth giving way to adult teeth, a necklace of white. He was alone, as usual. He asked me to shoot penalties at him. His heart was set on being a goalie, but the village team didn't want him. They call me 'The Sieve' because everything passes through, he said; and it struck me that a madman and a sieve might make the perfect combination. So I agreed and he jumped for joy. I'd seen Léon do the same little jump the first time we invited his best friend for a sleepover. I let the little goalie lead me several streets away from the square, to a small cul-de-sac. Goalposts and a net had been drawn on the mud wall at one end, along with the usual crude words and phrases. It's dead easy, you shoot from here, and I'll go over there, I'm Jorge Campos. The first time I took a shot at goal I almost broke my toes. He didn't stop the ball, but I had sent it

a good three metres over the crossbar. The second time I shot more carefully, almost gently; it was an easier ball to stop. And he stopped it. The third was trickier. Into the top corner. The Sieve jumped, but the ball hit the wall behind him. He fell over, then got up, rubbing his shoulder with a little manly frown.

The fourth kick, the fifth, all the way up to the twentieth were painful both for my foot and for the goalie's honour. The villagers came to watch. There were oohs and aahs, applause and laughter. A farmer offered to take over from me. Jorge Campos stopped two good balls. I was getting ready to shoot for the last time when a female voice called to the child. Arginaldo! He ran off. That's my sister, he told me as he ran past, I have to go home. I turned around. His sister was a good deal older than he was. She had very deep, dark eyes. Then Arginaldo returned to me for barely half a second.

Thanks, *El loco*.

The Pacific – violent and fascinating – the beauty of the place, the thousands of birds, the gentle air, the absence of a telephone, fax or the internet, of electricity, of bad news coming from the outside world, all those things go some way to explaining why the Desconocido is never empty. When guests leave they are immediately replaced by new guests. They come from Delhi, San Francisco, Hamburg, Birkirkara, Moscow, Cape Town. They arrive careworn and leave happy. Some couples don't leave their *palafito*. Others walk all day beside the ocean. They are given the most marvellous picnics. They return in the evening with red cheeks, their skin dry and salty. Some have been birdwatching. One of them spotted a great kiskadee, a laughing gull and some great egrets. Others were lucky enough to see sea turtles hatching, and helped them to the warm water. They saved the turtles' lives. They talk about it in the evenings, wonder-struck, their fevered eyes shining in the candlelight.

A few months ago I was one of them. In the evening, I would listen to the Norwegian couple telling me about their passion for Thoreau, and we would have heated discussions late into the night. Students came back late, gently drunk. Idealism. Cowardice. Nature. Industrialisation, the absence of meaning. I talked about the horsemeat found in French lasagne. The shit found in some biscuits. No one believed me. We ordered more champagne. The flames of the candles made the bubbles dance, made our eyelids flutter. Some light from La Tour. Then darkness, just a metre away. Threats.

We seemed to be at the very end of the world, a place where everything stops. Where you discover that the Earth isn't round. That a few miles away, the ocean falls away like a cascade, the water disappearing off into space, each drop becoming a tiny star. We are so small, we're already finished. Léon never asked me why the Earth is round. Why don't the people who live at the South Pole fall off, Papa?

I've been offered evening work at the hotel, on top of my cleaning. On those evenings I earn another sixty pesos. At this rate, after three hundred and eighty nights, I'll be able to buy myself a second-hand Beetle. I clear the tables after the last guests go to bed. I wash the dishes. I laugh with Pascual. He claims to have slept with almost a thousand women. Eight hundred and seventy-three to be precise. Not a Parisienne among them, but he doesn't mind that. He's been told the women of Paris aren't *golosa* in bed. Greed is what he likes in love, and in bed. I set the tables for breakfast. When my work is done, I sleep outside on the sand next to the vast ocean, so full of fish; I sleep for a few warm hours. The sound of the ocean lulls me. It is warm, hoarse, like the breathing of a father. But a courageous father, this time.

'Yes, exactly. Tell me about your father?'

'It's hard to talk about him. He's dying, of cancer. Cancer of the colon and the liver. The last time they checked, it had spread to one of his lungs. It's inoperable. But he's acting like he's blind to it all. Maybe to spare his wife's feelings, but mainly so he doesn't have to fight it. I don't think that makes me sad. I'm sad about my mother. I was devastated when she died. She died a furious death. It was the year Léon was born. The year Nathalie was unfaithful to me again. All of a sudden I was orphaned. I felt disgusted by myself, not just mentally but physically too. I felt as if I stank, like a piece of shit. People were leaving me. Everyone was leaving me. And Léon didn't need me yet, he didn't need a father at all. His mother gave him everything he needed. With the other man's smell on her, his pathetic scent, the stale smell of sex. I tried not to be jealous. That's the good thing about cowards: they don't protest. Like my father before me. Well, you did want me to talk about him.' (Here he gets up and opens the window wider because of my cigarettes. But he doesn't complain.) 'I remember thinking that my father was good-looking when he told women in the pharmacy that he would find a solution to their problems. My sister and I used to watch him through the window of Lapchin's pharmacy. And we felt proud. For those few moments we were wonderfully happy — why aren't happiness and rain-bows built to last? There's a solution for everything, Madame Michel; a solution just for you, Madame Doré. And they would look at him as though he were Jesus. 'For everyone that asketh receiveth.'* He was making them happy, and he knew it. They loved him for it. So why didn't he rescue us, too? Why were his solutions only for other people? Why did he allow our mother to leave?' (Here I heave a sigh of exasperation.) 'Excuse me.' (I stub out my cigarette.) 'Yes, it's really shit to have inherited all this stuff. That's what I hold against him. It wasn't just that he didn't love us enough to rescue us — and he loved his bloody customers enough for that. It's that he made me become the same as him. A piece of shit, a coward. He should have hit me and

* St Luke, 11.5–13.

shouted: I don't want you to be like me, Antoine, do you hear me? Ever! Don't become like me, stay away from me! My mother had warned me, but I hadn't understood. It's a father's job to tell you things like that. One day when he was trying to park the car, someone else nipped into the slot ahead of him. Smash his face in, Papa, I thought, smash his face in, don't let him screw you over. But he said nothing. He just put the car in first, drove off and dropped me at home, without saying a word. I swore to myself, then, that things like that wouldn't happen to me when I was grown up. And then they did. He passed his condition on to me. I grew up with that sense of shame. The worst thing was being ashamed of myself. I know he'd like to come and see me. But right now I don't want that. I'm not ready for it. The damage I've done is the damage he did.'

On the evenings when I went back to El Tuito, Arginaldo and I met to continue his training. Being short didn't stop Jorge Campos becoming the greatest goalkeeper of all time, Arginaldo told me. I kicked the ball hard enough to sprain my ankle. Every evening The Sieve flew higher, flew further, dived faster, fumed louder and cursed harder, and sometimes he gave himself a round of applause. After three months, he had gone from conceding ninety-four goals out of a hundred to conceding only seventy-one. A very encouraging figure, I reassured him. And believe me, my aim was getting better all the time.

When he got it down to sixty-five out of a hundred, he gave me a pair of Nikes. He had come to sit beside me after our training session as I coughed up my lungs. He put his small hand on my shoulder. I have a present for you. My sister paid, but it was my idea. To say thank you. Here. They're almost the same as Kakà's. And then, in a lower voice: I'd love to have trainers like his. Some day.

I began to laugh. And to sob at the same time. I hugged the boy. I was shaking. I suddenly wanted to make promises. Reunions. I wanted the pleasure of that. I'll give you some when you're grown up, Arginaldo. You won't be here when I'm grown up. Why do you say that? My sister says. She says you won't stay here, you'll leave. Because that's always what happens.

So I took the shoes that were like Kakà's Nikes and put them on. Then I stood up, and I jogged on the spot five or six times before jumping up as high as I could. When I landed, the studs sank entirely into the ochre soil.

Twenty-four little roots.

I'm going to stay here, Arginaldo. I promise. I'm going to stay here, and you're going to become the best goalkeeper in the world.

'Let's get back to your father. You told me that he recently said he regretted not having driven you to see Patricia V* after, after — let me look at my notes — after you dined together at the *Café de la Gare*, and that you had wondered why we only meet the people who have been missing from our lives just as we are losing them.'

'I don't know what to say. He's nearly seventy-five. The medication he's on must be dulling his wits. He has a wife who talks all the time and never stops to take a breath. He's suffocating. He must be terrified. I imagine he retreats into himself, perhaps he finds islands there: beaches of silence; things that can be forgiven. He's in denial, but he knows he's on the way out. I'm sure his memories are resurfacing. Memories that scare him. Maybe he wanted to tell me something. To say he remembered that evening, and understood how much the girl had mattered to me.'

'Maybe he wanted to tell you that you mattered to him.'

4×4

The pick-up truck stops dead, in a cloud of dust, in the middle of the road. On the flatbed at the back of the truck, we're all thrown against each other. There are cries and cracking sounds. A day labourer is thrown clear out of the truck. He gets up, laughing, then passes out when he sees his left forearm jutting from his elbow at an alarming angle. The women hurry over to him. The driver, his face bleeding, raises his arms to the heavens, disfigured by his fury. He looks under the 4×4. He looks at both sides of the road. Nothing. Now he is proclaiming, *¡Espíritu maligno! ¡Espíritu maligno!* As the day labourer comes back to his senses and the women finish wedging his twisted arm into a small wooden splint, I walk to the front of the big Toyota. Pascual is there with me, rubbing his shoulder, which had slammed into the cab. I walk around the pick-up. The driver is sitting about ten metres from us now, repeating *¡Espíritu* *maligno!* As the dust falls back to earth, he is covered; it makes him look like a ghost.

I find myself being propelled back five years. To a time when my mind was trying to explain the inexplicable. To the instinct I used to have in those days. I was the ultimate bastard, the little guy who had to find the flaw in the story he'd been told so the company wouldn't have to pay up. I tell the others to take the front wheels off the truck. I smile. I knew it. The pistons and hydraulic chamber of the front brakes have both been replaced by Chinese or Korean fakes. The fake steel has melted, causing a piston to jam, thereby more or less sticking the brake pads to the disc, causing the pick-up to stop suddenly; causing the right angle in the day labourer's arm, the ghostly look of the driver, and the women's screams.

I take the front brakes apart, neutralise the liquid intake, and check that the back brakes are working. Then I put the two large front wheels back on the truck. Pascual is watching me like a child, even though he is old enough to be my father. *El loco*, you astonish me! You have a golden touch, and here you are working as a cleaner. We turn round and drive slowly down the road to El Tuito, heading for the Health Centre. The day labourer groans as he lies among us, on a tarpaulin that scrapes his back. One woman is stroking his forehead like a mother. Another is praying.

Pascual takes my hand and examines it as if it were a precious stone. You're a doctor. You can cure *things*.

He is holding the hand that shot my daughter five years before.

'Do you still think about death?'

'No.'

'What did you want to do away with that night?'

'The curse.'

'Did you think about the people who would be left behind? About their grief?'

'My need for peace was greater. I thought they would understand.'

'Would understand what?'

'To understand is to take a step towards someone, a giant step. It's the beginning of forgiveness.'

'You wanted to be forgiven for what you'd planned to do?'

'No, I just wanted them to understand that I had no other way out.'

'You didn't want to be forgiven?'

'That would have been impossible. Recently a

couple killed both their children then hanged themselves. They left a note. *This isn't a murder it's an act of
love*. Who can understand that? Forgiveness doesn't
apply to people like that. It's fear that overcomes
you.'

'You say you had no other way out.'

'Nothing else seemed to matter, compared to the
fear.'

'Was that the wild beast you mentioned?'

'At a certain point, it overwhelmed me. It was in
control. You know there's going to be carnage, but you
also know a time will come when it will all be over.
When you won't have to suffer any more.'

'Why Joséphine and Léon?'

'I was afraid.'

'Afraid?'

'I told myself that if they never woke up again,
nothing bad could happen to them.'

'Like your sister Anne?'

'Like my sister Anne.'

'Did you never wonder whether Anne would rather
have lived, if she'd had the choice?'

'Questions like that don't lead anywhere.'

'That's for me to decide.'

'I think she liked being alive. I suppose she'd have
wanted to live, like Anna.'

'And your children, don't you think they would have liked to live, too?'

'The divorce was making them suffer a great deal.'

'It happens to many children.'

'Léon had been wetting the bed again. Joséphine wasn't doing well at school. They thought she had attention deficit syndrome. Both the children were seeing a psychologist. Nathalie had been offered a better job in Lyon. She was going to move there with the artistic director. They'd have been seven hundred kilometres away. We wouldn't have been able to see each other any more, or touch, or spend time together. They didn't want that kind of life.'

'Did you ask them?'

'I didn't want that kind of life for them.'

'But you had lost your job, didn't you think about moving to Lyon, too? You could have made a new start there.'

'I wasn't going to change my life to suit a woman who'd cheated on me and was walking out on me.'

'I'm talking about your children.'

'I didn't have the strength.'

'Wasn't it more because your children hadn't chosen you? Because they were going with their mother? So you felt abandoned yet again? First by your mother, then by your wife. By your employer a few months before, and now by your father. It was all starting again, wasn't it? You told me, the other day, that you had left your mother – sorry, you hadn't gone to look for her in Bagnolet – because she didn't love you.'

'Love is a killer, too.'

'The absence of love, you mean.'

'The absence of love.'

'Why that particular night?'

'It had been a wonderful week. Nathalie was in Leucate with her lover, taking photos for their autumn catalogue. The children were staying with me. That last day had been particularly good. We had listened to music and danced in the living room. We'd made plans for a swimming pool in the garden. We went to eat cake at the Montois bakery, where my parents first held hands, where all the violence began. I wanted to change the course of events. To start again, from the place where everything started to go wrong, to obliterate that first lie. After lunch, Joséphine told me about what she wanted to study. Things she wanted to make. It was so lovely. We were profoundly happy.'

'You didn't stop to think those moments of happiness could be repeated?'

'I thought that evening would make a good ending.'

'Do you still think about death?'

'No.'

17

One Sunday we go to the beach at Mayto, to the south of Puerto Vallarta. Pascual is driving the van. Three of the hotel's cleaning ladies are with us, along with the husband of one and the fiancé of another. The women have made an enormous salad of lentils and chickpeas. And guacamole. The men have contributed several bottles of Nebbiolo. Arginaldo has brought his football, which has been mended so many times. The beach is magnificent. Huge. Seventeen kilometres long. The road there is bumpy, to discourage tourists. There is one small hotel, which is always half empty. And a sanctuary for sea turtles abandoned by their mothers.

The ocean is rougher here and the braver visitors love the strong wind as they surf. It is said that some take off and never come back to earth. Others are swallowed up by the ocean and are washed ashore, weeks later, their bodies contorted and bloated. They wash up in the tiny port of Tehuamixtle, a few kilometres away. The ocean disfigures those who want to tame it, and threatens everyone else.

While four of us play football, Pascual stays with the women. He makes them laugh. Arginaldo is having the time of his life; he is having a wonderful day. We all are.

After our meal, the wine makes us sleepy. Pascual is snoring, with his head on the breast of the third cleaning lady, Dominga. She is a widow. He dreams of her becoming his eight hundred and seventy-fourth conquest. He wants to make them all happy because he once wronged a woman. Dominga gently strokes his hair like an elder sister. The engaged couple have gone off towards a little creek, blushing. Arginaldo is doing combinations with his ball. Chest-knee-head. Head-foot-knee. I am dozing.

I see us again with Anna, as children, beside Lake Lauvitel, at Bourg-d'Oisans, before all this.

Before I thought nothing good could ever happen again. Before the terrifying moment when I ran out of strength, when I would lie down on the ground and weep, letting my tears carry me away.

I get to my feet.

I walk into the warm ocean. I move through its enchanting colours. Every shade of blue: turquoise, azure, Bondi blue, Mayan blue, aquamarine, Tiffany blue. I advance. The water is up to my knees. Suddenly I feel that I am sinking, and I allow myself to sink. A powerful wave arrives and sweeps me backwards while the backwash sucks me down. Tiny pebbles hit my back. The choppy waters take me prisoner. I pull my feet from the heavy sand. My body is like a shuttlecock, light and resisting control. It is whirling. I can't tell where the surface of the water is, which way is up. For a moment my head rises above the water, and I have just enough time to see Arginaldo's face, his frantic gestures. I can't hear what he is shouting. I am sucked in again, battered and beaten. I utter a cry but the ocean drowns it instantly. I push out my hands and my feet. I am a little turtle, I have to survive. I make for the light. The surface. I am thrown out, disgorged. My forehead hits the sharp edge of a stone. Arginaldo tugs at my arms, trying to pull me from the water. He isn't strong enough. He shouts, weeps, sniffles. Pascual comes running. At last I am on the beach, the boy on all fours beside me. He takes my face in his hands; he is trembling. You said you'd stay! You said you'd stay! I smile at him. I stroke his terrified face, and wipe away his silver tears.

I'm here, Arginaldo. I'll stay with you.

I have fought. I have chosen life.

3

When we got back to El Tuito, Arginaldo insisted that I go home with him. My sister trained as a nurse. She'll see to your forehead. She once stitched my knee up, and it didn't hurt.

Matilda made me sit down in the kitchen so she could soften the encrusted blood with warm water, while the little footballer told her about the rescue, my fight against the ocean, my victory. You should have seen *El loco*, it was just like Erik Morales.* Now that I was safe and sound, he mimed the dives he'd made on the sand, the way he'd deflected the shots. The crockery on the table almost went flying several times. His sister smiled. She had a lovely smile. Her dark eyes met mine, but did not linger. She disinfected the cut and examined it. Then

* Mexican boxer, world bantamweight champion (1997–2000), featherweight champion (2001–2003), and super-featherweight champion (2004).

at last she spoke: three stitches if you want to stay *guapo*, only one if you want to be *golfo*. Arginaldo burst out laughing. Say three stitches, *El loco*, she hates a man who's *golfo! Golfo* means thuggish, *guapo* is handsome.

Her hands did not shake. Nor did I. Not when the needle went into my skin, when the thread stretched it, nor when she looked at me, for longer this time and announced: It's done. It's done, and I want to thank you for everything you're doing for my brother. You've taught him how to laugh again. It would give me pleasure if you would stay to eat with us. At this Arginaldo did his little jump, the one like Léon's. A little jump of triumph.

In the time it took her to prepare the meal I went back to my room and showered my salty, scraped skin. I changed out of my T-shirt and into a white shirt – Arginaldo will laugh at me, I thought; you look like you're going to church, he will say.

I went to buy her a present. As I chose from the hundred on offer, my heart was racing. Yet there was nothing between us. No ambiguity. I had only seen her twice. I had been struck by her dark eyes, which were piercing and mysterious. There was resignation in her gentle, sad expression. A sense of distance. A beauty that would not show itself.

Did she have her own demons?

The little goalie hugged me, and then embraced me hysterically when I threw him a brand-new ball. It was almost like Ronaldinho's. Matilda lowered her eyes and the blood rose to her cheeks when I gave her a bracelet made out of pink and black stone beads. My fingers trembled as I helped her fasten it around her wrist. You'd make a terrible nurse, she said, laughing. Her laughter reassured me and I joined in. It seemed as if I was finally ridding myself of something. Shedding an old skin, an old smell. I had not been close to a woman since Nathalie, I had felt only disgust.

During the three years I spent in shackles, at one remove from the world, I had clung to the journalist's sublime sadness. It was my lifeline, my beautiful lifeline. It had allowed me to survive, to bear the whiteness, the cold, the steel. The bars on the windows. The tubes of silvery fluid. I had imagined bringing her here. Or somewhere else. Every day for three years I had dreamed of a new life for us. I would banish her sadness and my grief. When I was feverish, I sometimes heard peals of laughter. Sometimes our skin touched, her lips brushed my ear, speaking words of passion. But if anything was to come of such dreams, the other person would want to be dreamed about. She had simply put down the phone, she had hung up on me, and I hadn't been sad. Her silence had awoken me.

You have a nice laugh, Matilda told me. It makes people want to laugh with you.

And I felt close to tears. Everything has become so simple, I thought, so real. I kept her wrist in my hand for a moment, and she did not immediately withdraw it. She looked down at her bracelet. It's lovely, she said, those colours are unusual here, you know. There's much more red, yellow and orange.

I.

Her wrist rises in the air, light and elegant, as she sweeps a lock of hair from her forehead.

I.

I think we should eat, she murmurs. Her dark eyes do not meet mine. Let's sit down, shall we? Arginaldo! The hint of a delightful smile dances around her mouth. It lasts for barely a tenth of a second, but that is enough to show me her great beauty. The light she has hidden from the world for more than eight years.

46

The *pozolo blanco* was perfect. A casserole of pork with cacahuazintle sweetcorn, a white kind of corn that opens up as the grains cook, forming little flowers on the plate. Arginaldo made us laugh by imitating Jared Borgetti, the striker who had scored forty-six goals for the national team. The stories he told about school moved us. Matilda did not tuck her hair behind her ears. Sometimes she glanced at the bracelet I had given her. Our eyes did not meet – because her little brother was there, I suppose. She, in turn, told anecdotes about her work at the Health Centre. That mariachi player, totally *borracho*, who had stuck his violin bow in his eye. It was horrible. Arginaldo thought it was hilarious. He had mimed a drunken mariachi, moving like a zombie. It was awful, it's not nice to laugh, Arginaldo, it's not very Christian. We laughed even more. Our laughter was as warm as a fire, with flames that made our eyes water.

Then it was time for Arginaldo to go to bed. He took my hand and led me to his bedroom. Tell me a story, *El loco*. Please. My sister always tells the same ones.

Sitting on the bed beside him, I told him the stories I used to read to Joséphine and Léon. About children getting the better of monsters. Breaking magic spells. Bringing the stars down from the heavens. The story of the man who brought home the sun. The story of the woman who turned into a vixen. The story of the seven lost brothers. The trials and tribulations of a straight line.

In the shadows, Matilda listened. I enjoyed that quiet, gentle moment. We had no past, no future. Only the heady sensation of a moment of grace, a moment which asked for nothing, expected nothing.

Matilda walked me to the door. In less than four hours' time, the van would come to take me to the Desconocido. We took a few steps into the warm night. The tiny stone beads glistened on her wrist. We said nothing. It seemed to me that we were adjusting our pace to keep in time with each other, and that made us laugh. Two little bursts of laughter stifled by the weight of the darkness.

We have our own language, already.

At the end of the road we parted. The green of my eyes plunged into the dark night of hers. We said what we had to say.

'The job centre months were a nightmare. Like something out of Kafka. The people there didn't understand a single thing. They didn't listen. They hid behind their little desks, their little screens; their little pride in having a job, in thinking they were important. Their salary comes out of our taxes. Their retirement ruins us. They forget that. They have no compassion, no tenderness. No tact whatsoever. I've seen them stop in the middle of an interview because it was time to knock off. It was four bloody thirty. People were in tears because their lives had been ruined, and the job centre people went off to have their tea. Come back tomorrow, we open at 8.30 a.m. Exactly when the kids are being taken to school. So when you get to the centre, you have to queue for four hours. Everyone's nerves were all over the place. It felt like war. They offered me anything and everything. Painting car bodywork.

Welding. Sound engineering. That's all we have right now. The car industry's finished. They've extorted so much money from people with cars that now they are walking. Try selling shoes or bicycles, train to be something else. Spare us your pathetic complaints. A thousand more on the dole every day. It's you or someone else. You can shout all you like, what do you expect us to do? You want to replace me, do you? You want my job? Come on, then, come on! Stop, or I'll call security. You make me want to puke. There was always something missing from my file. They asked me about twenty times to produce my pay slips for the last year. For five years. A certificate I'd sent them three times already, that they'd lost three times. We changed our software, so sorry. Sorry, my arse. They do it to make you feel nauseous, to make you crack up. That's one less person on the dole. The curve is inverted. Lies win the day. I've been waiting for my redundancy payment for eight months – nothing. And just think, Nathalie's kicking up a fuss. Her whole salary's running through her fingers, going down the drain. But it wasn't just that. She had a man in Paris, she was sleeping at the Terminus Nord hotel. I was alone. She had a babysitter for the children. I was having sleepless nights, drinking, dealing with my father's cancer. And the obese plumbers. All those humiliations. By the time I reached that point, I wanted to give the finger to a world I'd stopped liking. A world that didn't like me back. But I was incapable even of that. So I decided that my cowardice, my disappointment, and my weakness, all of that would end with me. I wouldn't pass it on. I wanted it to dry up, at source.'

'Was that the trigger?'

'When your romantic life is over, when your family is over and your social life is going the same way, you know that you are going over to the dark side. To a pitch-black place. A place where you won't be found. So, yes, maybe that was the trigger.'

El loco was no more. In less than two years I had become *El mago*, the magician.

The unfortunate, the unhappy and the indebted entrusted their cars to Pascual, and to my Midas touch. They gave us their pick-up trucks and vans. We gave them a special service. In the days that followed, airbags mysteriously went off. On straight roads, at red lights. Or simply when the ignition was switched on. The drivers suffered slight burns to their arms. Sometimes the detonations caused small lesions to their eardrums. The insurance companies and car manufacturers, wanting to avoid scandal at any cost, paid up without any argument.

A woman from Mascota received over a hundred and fifty thousand pesos; the skin of her cheek had been injured by her glasses. The bastard was changing sides. By slightly modifying the composition of perchlorate, the gas that inflates airbags, I was making the hyenas pay. I was avenging the pregnant women who had been abandoned. The people like Grzeskowiak, who loved their Yvette. The little people. I was washing my hands of the criminals I had known. The plumbers who stole from you. The taxi drivers who swindled you. The women who betrayed you. The father who gave you his sickness, only to give himself an equally mortal disease. The part of you that would not heal.

The *víctimas* pay Pascual and me a small percentage of the compensation they receive. However, I also carry on with my work as a cleaner at the Desconocido; it's my link to my mother's hands, the hands that I didn't feel enough.

I have bought a 1986 Beetle (without airbags) in perfect condition, and on Sundays I take Matilda for a drive along Highway 200. We drive without any destination in mind. She lets her arm hang out of the window; her fingers caress the warm breeze. Sometimes, for no reason, she laughs. And sometimes she cries.

Then I feel a chill.

First

Anna came to see me. We met in the visiting room. A guard was present. Her eyes misted over when she saw how pale and thin I was; the dark rings round my eyes as if they had been punched. *Oh God have done you.* Oh, my God, what have they done to you? I caressed her face. Her warmth and sweetness penetrated my hand. It was the first time I had touched another human being in nearly a year. A woman's skin. My fingers traced her cheekbones, passed over her cheek, stopping at her mouth and parting her lips. They were moist. Anna closed her eyes, leaning in to murmur her disjointed words to me. She was beautiful and desperate in the gift that she suddenly gave to me. My crude, obscene gesture brought me back into contact with life. My fingers slid into her mouth. I began to cry.

Then she told me about them. Our father was suffering terribly. He lay in bed most of the time. Morphine, vomiting; his bag of shit stuck to his hip. The shame of it. He was being fed through a drip. His tears never stopped flowing. His wife massaged him to prevent bed-sores, with miserable, inconsolable little movements, the final expressions of tenderness. He hardly spoke; at the deafening sound of the shot I'd fired his words had taken flight. That night, powerless and mute, he had witnessed his grandson's terror. It takes courage and so much love to save another person. He had not said, either to Léon or to me, the few phrases that would make rebirth possible. The trembling that afflicted my father's wife's mouth had spread to the rest of her body. She was like a piece of paper blowing in the wind, car-ried away on a last gust. They never talked about my madness, my animal darkness. Silence ignores things, attempts to make them go away. Anna visited our father and his wife regularly. Time was passing, with its foul odour. Cruel Death had invited itself in.

Nathalie and the children had gone to live in Lyon, with the tattooed guy. They were a family now. People passed the time of day with them in the street and thought the children beautiful, in spite of the girl's dis-figured cheek. Nothing was really known about them, none of the horror. They lived in a large apartment near the Tête-d'Or park. Nathalie had a good job, with a company car. Léon was doing all right. His nightmares were becoming few and far between; he was wetting his bed less frequently now. The results of the first skin graft on Joséphine's face were encouraging. There were plans for at least two more. Her rehabilitation was going all right; it would take a long time, but she was beginning to speak again. The words were no longer stuck in her wound; they no longer fell into the abyss excavated by my grief – apart from the word Papa, which had disappeared entirely. My children did not want to see me again. Ever. They had asked to change their surname, they wanted to be rid of me. They had burned all the photographs, all traces of my existence. They had obliterated me. They had killed me.

Then, at the end of the afternoon, when she was by the door and the guard was preparing to open it, Anna stood perfectly still for a moment, then turned towards me.

Joséphine asks same. So did decide shoot first. Joséphine always asks the same question. So why did he decide to shoot me first?

1,000

I remember the first time our father sent us to summer camp. He had said he would pack our suitcases, but he forgot to put a spare pair of trousers in mine.

At breakfast on the second morning, someone bumped into me by accident and I spilt my cup of hot chocolate all over my trousers. It left a shameful, dark patch on my crotch, which looked like the urine stains on my father's clothes today. The other children laughed. They said cruel, hurtful things about me. My tears only encouraged them. And when Anna desperately begged them, *it*, *it* (meaning 'stop it, stop it') they laughed even more.

I remember when my father sent me to buy underwear for my sister. He didn't dare do it himself. He always looked away when he passed the window of a lingerie shop. Particularly the shop in the Rue Alsace-Lorraine run by Madame Christiane.

He never held hands with us in the street.

He never talked about Anne.

He never lay on our beds in the evening to tell us stories. He never made up stories. Sometimes he bought a book, but he never read it to us. I remember *Hansel and Gretel*. I must have read it to Anna a thousand times. My sour saliva had nibbled away at the corners of the pages and they stank. But it was our story, our book. Every time she heard it, my sister pulled the quilt right up to her nose. Every time it made her tremble.

He never cried over photos of our mother. He just drank beer until his head fell onto his plate.

He didn't know the names of trees, or flowers, or birds. Only the names of chemical formulas. Those names do not bring humans closer; they do not start conversations.

He never listened to music. He never taught us to cry when we listened to Mahler. He never taught us to cry, full stop. Or how to express our grief.

Our joy.

Our anger.

He never lay in the grass so he could look up at the sky.

He never ate a worm. He was never stung by a wasp.

He never punched anyone in the face.

He never took us for a walk in the rain.

Never had a snowball fight with us.

He never took us to the swimming pool, never splashed about in the water, never played at who could stay underwater the longest.

He never sent us letters when we were at summer camp. Later, when Nathalie left me, he never picked up the phone to call me.

He always forgot the school fête.

He never ran after a football with me, or chased a tennis ball, or a ping-pong ball.

Never chased a dream.

Or a feather flying through the air.

He always went to buy chocolate cakes from the Montois bakery on a Sunday.

He always got the dates of our birthday wrong. He gave Anna the same present twice.

He never bought presents for my children. His wife did that.

He never talked about his parents. About the Algerian war. About his fears when he grew up, his dreams, his life before us. Before all this.

One day he took me to see *Papillon* at the Palace cinema and when a convict was guillotined he put his hands over my eyes. We never went to the cinema together again.

He never taught me how to shave.

He never talked to me about girls, their stomachs, their hearts, their bodies.

Or about the violence of men.

He never told me I was good-looking. Or ugly. Tall. Short. Fat. Thin.

Never told a funny story.

He believed in Paradise, maybe.

He said he liked songs by Serge Reggiani. He never went to hear him live. And now Serge Reggiani is dead.

2

One day I asked him to teach me how to fish. There were ponds full of fish in Masnières, a few kilometres away: trout, roach, gudgeon. He heaved a sigh. There are two fishmongers in town, he told me. But Papa, I persisted, we're going fishing with school in two weeks' time, and I've never been fishing, I'll look silly again.

There's no need to feel silly about something like that, Antoine.

I exploded. You look silly, I cried, you look silly. I can still hear my thin, trembling voice, like a sparrow chirping, *You look silly, you look silly*, my words scraping the kitchen walls. I shouted louder. I wish you were the one who left.

He buried his face in his hands. His shoulders drooped; that was his specialty. I felt terribly ashamed of him, and I swore to myself that I would never be a father like him.

I was even worse.

It was a good, hard kick. The ball whistled through the air. The spectators fell silent. The little goalkeeper was rooted to the spot. He reacted a quarter of a second too late. The ball smashed into his face with the force of a cannonball. His frail body toppled backwards. There was shouting. Cries of delight broke out on the other side of the pitch when the ball and child's body fell over the line. The referee whistled with all his might, as if his whistle could hold the body upright, could stop it falling.

Then people came running, among them a male nurse from the Health Centre. The child's nose was broken and he had a wobbly tooth. The boy stayed on the ground for a moment, feeling groggy. When they wanted to carry him off the pitch he refused. He insisted on standing up and walking off himself. Once he was on his feet, his face bleeding, he raised his arms to make a large V. Everyone applauded.

That goal brought the score to one–all. Thirty minutes remained on the clock. Confusion reigned, because the team had no substitute goalie but the rules said that the game must go on.

There was an animated discussion among the team, which was now one man short. No one offered to be in goal. Play without a goalie, the referee suggested. Be *magníficos*. I'll give you another two minutes and then I'm restarting the game. Otherwise it's *retirarse*, forfeit.

I got out of my seat and approached the young footballers to make a proposition. They shrugged. Two of them sniggered.

Not him. Not The Sieve. We'll lose ten-one.

Well? asked the referee.

OK, but if we lose, you must promise to buy us new shoes.

I promise. All of you.

And so Arginaldo went onto the pitch, to the sound of booing. The match resumed. Matilda's dark eyes were fixed on mine, and then on my lips. Her fingers brushed my fingers. Their gentle message said thank you. Their butterfly lightness spoke of her fear and her relief.

On the field, her brother's team stepped up their efforts to keep the other side away from the goal defended by The Sieve. It was an aggressive tactic, and it worked. Six minutes from the end – when Arginaldo still hadn't touched the ball – they scored a second goal. And still they didn't let up. But here came one of the other side's players, an eel, like Maradona in his prime. He took possession, dribbled like a devil, and then ran towards the goal that Arginaldo was guarding. Only one defender remained between the ball and The Sieve. Then the defender tripped up the attacking player. Within the eighteen-yard box.

Penalty.

The celebrations went on late into the night. The men drank a great deal of *raicilla*, fermented agave. A devious spirit that had been known to topple even the sturdiest of men. Tables were improvised and salads were brought. Chicken was grilled, *fajitas* made. Musicians plucked the strings of their guitars and violins. Women danced, the sound of their song cutting through the night; passions ran high. Matilda laughed, her eyes shining with a dark, mysterious fire. A man invited her to dance the *quebradita*. She stopped laughing and flinched as if she had been burnt. She declined. When our gaze met, she lowered her eyes. I went over to her. I finally dared to ask. Don't worry, I'm no good at dancing. She burst out laughing. But that's what you do with Arginaldo. Look at how happy he is, how full of life.

Further away, about twenty metres from us, there was hysteria. The little football team surrounded the boy, applauding him, celebrating his achievement, while for the umpteenth time that night he demonstrated the dive that had blocked the ball, saved the penalty, secured the victory. I did what *El mago* told me, he said. Look into the eyes of the man taking the ball and you'll see the direction in which it will come. He looked to his right so I dived to my left.

After that triumphant save, the boys had rushed over to The Sieve, hauled him out of goal, and carried him aloft like a trophy. Then the referee had blown the whistle for the end of the game. Just over three years since we first began his training in a blind alleyway, Arginaldo was becoming one of the best goalies in the world.

When her brother saved the ball, Matilda squeezed my hand. She didn't want to cry. Happiness is so intoxicating, so violent, that it sweeps everything else away. Including shame and fear. Just like unhappiness, it can cut deep, it can make you falter, it can destroy you. But no one ever says that, in case we lose our faith in happiness. Because then the world would collapse. Then we would all be wild beasts, devouring one another.

Later, Arginaldo ran towards us, exhausted, dusty and stiff. His small arms brought us together, making, for a moment, a single body of us all.

And at last I understood what I had been missing all along.

Day dawned, illuminating the shadowy corners where men slept tangled up together, their minds dulled by alcohol and laughter. Sometimes their faces were scratched by the women who had refused them. There were exhausted bodies all the way to the Rosita arcades. For the first time in sixteen years, the *niños* of El Tuito had beaten the team from Las Juntas, which left in tears, straight after the match. The losing team, aged from eight to twelve, would grow up in the shadow of that defeat. Before boarding the bus, the boy who had looked to the right when he took the penalty shouted: My father's going to murder me, my father's going to murder me! Then Arginaldo gave the boy his football, the one that I had given him, and that had brought him luck. I felt proud. Like a father.

Day dawned and, like Pascual and Dominga – who hadn't yet fallen for Pascual's charms – I had missed the van to the Desconocido. I went home with Matilda and her brother. For the first time, Arginaldo called me by my first name. Antonio. Matilda invited me in. I slept on the sofa, buried under a feather quilt. Drowned. Happy.

When I surfaced in the afternoon, Matilda was sitting looking at me.

We were not afraid any more.

9

A few weeks later, Arginaldo and his sister invited me to come and live with them. Say yes, Antonio. Please say yes. For the price of my cell – ten pesos – they offered me a room just as tiny. But it had an adjoining kitchen, a sitting room (with television) a few feet away, and a terrace (or rather a chair with a cushion that sat in front of the house). We would eat together and laugh together. Say yes, Antonio, please say yes. We'd tell stories in the evening and do football practice on the street. You can teach us French, Antonio, and I'll teach you to cook. When it gets cold in winter we'll light a fire. If you are wounded I will stitch you back together again. I understood that in mending my broken heart she was mending her own, and her brother's. Matilda wanted to join us together and make us stronger.

One morning, when we were on our way to the Desconocido, I asked Pascual why Matilda had never married. He raised his eyes to the heavens and spat out the word *Fieras*.

Wild beasts.

The *niña* had been studying to be a nurse. This was just over nine years ago. Sometimes she'd help out at the Health Centre in the evenings. One night, two men came in. They'd been bottled in a summertime brawl, a drunkards' dance. In the treatment room the first man grabbed her. Then the second. No one heard her cries because she didn't cry out. When they had finished she was red all over, covered in their blood. She scrubbed her skin, wiped away their poisonous saliva, their salty sperm, their vulgar words, their greasy fingers. Then she went home. She gave up her studies. She stopped wanting to help people, to try to save them. She let her youth fade, she lost her laugh. She had a lovely laugh, Antonio, a really lovely laugh. Then she went to stay with her family in Puerto Vallarta for a while. When she came back here she said her mother had died, and the baby was her brother. People believed her. And there you go. How do you know this story, Pascual? I was there that night, but I was frightened. I hid. Don't judge me, Antonio. You've hidden too, you've been afraid. I've seen the fear in your eyes. You may have washed them a thousand times since you came here, but I can still see a trace. I've felt the same fears as you. I wanted to hide, bury myself in women. Make them happy, every last one, because of the woman I had abandoned. Your hiding place is silence. But silence is like the bullets from a revolver, Antonio. You can't keep them quiet and you can never stop them.

So then I told him everything; I told him about my demons, my wild beasts. My hand touched his and I felt the warm, thick, cracked skin that sent women mad. It was the hand of a man, of a father. It was huge. One by one, the words came: the names of my children, my father's cowardice, my mother's flight, her terrifying cough, Anne's eternal night, the noise of me punching my childhood bedroom walls, Nathalie's laughter when she came home at dawn smelling of another man, the sound of the job-centre staff knocking off at teatime. And all those words flew off and disappeared into the dust, like a wicked wind, blowing towards Mictlán, the realm of the dead.

Pascual held me close. I smelled his breath, sour, like a fermented apple. Both parties need to be wounded in order to meet, he murmured. Both must be wanderers, both must be lost souls. Otherwise the strong soul will crush the other, and end up killing it.

You two, you will save each other.

1 50,000 (continued)

Another winter has come. It has been seven years since the night of the wild beast. My children have grown up without me, just as I grew up without my mother. With everything crooked. Perhaps Nathalie has left her tattooed lover. Perhaps she has given him a child. Perhaps she has got rid of other men, other babies.

Nothing remains of those we miss except the absence we feel. In my memory, the faces of Joséphine and Léon blur, just as Anne's face has faded. All that remains are images, born of my fear of being entirely abandoned, entirely alone. But images can deceive. I still hear laughter in a garden, unsure whether that laughter really did exist. I remember a little blue coat as a little red coat. A flash of bright light on a sunless day. The colour of my father's eyes. The small impressionist touches that make up the album of our sorrows.

I had been tempted, once, to ask my sister to send

me photographs or news of them. But I decided against it.

I had never talked about them here. Except to Pascual.

Here I have learned to say goodbye to my dead. Time has put me back together again.

One morning a dusty, battered Chevrolet Astra stopped outside our workshop. When he recognised the driver, Pascual immediately thought there would be trouble. But the wide smile of the woman who got out of the little car quickly reassured us. Epifania Florès Alonso. She had come from Mescato, with a very discreet scar on her left cheekbone where the lens of her glasses had been smashed by the airbag of her car. The insurance company had paid her more than 150,000 pesos, and her husband had begun to dream of keeping her windfall without keeping her. So I'd like to know, Señor Antonio, whether your golden fingers could do something to his electric shaver, something that would cut his throat, that big vein in his neck, so his blood pours out like a *chancho*. What a bastard. I'll give you money. At this, Pascual took her in his arms, the arms that had made eight hundred and seventy-three women dance – not counting Dominga, who was still being coy. He whispered in her ear words that are usually sung, an old mariachi ballad about an angry madman who killed his beloved with three bullets, and the heart of his beloved bled and wept, and the heart asked him: Why didn't you just run away, why, Epifania, there's no love where there is anger. Epifania Florès Alonso felt her heart lifting and wiped away the tear that was slowly trickling down her scar. I understand, Pascual, she said, sniffling, you have opened my eyes. *Gracias. Gracias.* And as for you, Señor Antonio, save your beautiful hands for beautiful things.

3

'I'd like us to talk about something you mentioned several weeks ago, because it strikes me as important.' (He looks through his notes. I light a cigarette. The first puff is always a delicious moment.) 'Ah, here we are. You went to see your father, you watched a film, *Singin' in the Rain*. You were spending time with him; it was your way of saying goodbye. Then you went to see your sister and her husband, again for the last time, before shooting your children and then yourself, or at least that was your plan. And as you were leaving, Anna said: Choose the day. I'd like you to go back over those words.'

'It's funny you mention that. Those three words have haunted me for a long time. You know that my sister and I had a very close relationship after Anne's death. Before Thomas came into our lives, I was the only one who could understand her half-sentences.

When Anne died, we took each other by the hand; we protected one another from the violence and abandonment of our childhood. And I ended up thinking she knew me better than I knew myself. There was no way she couldn't have noticed the wild beast. She knew it would come out, and by coming out it would liberate me, it would liberate us all, and that there wasn't any other option for me. I had lost everything. My wife, my work, my children's respect. I thought that by saying what she said – choose the day – she was giving me her blessing, telling me: go on, do it now, choose a date, do what you have to do, I understand and I forgive you, you are my brother and I will always love you, no matter what.'

'So?'

'So, that wasn't what she meant.' (I am silent for a moment. I don't want to cry. I breathe from the pit of my stomach.) 'She meant *Choose the day*. Choose the light, not the shade where wild beasts live. That was what she wanted to say. Choose some other way. Go towards the unknown. Towards life.' (I light another cigarette. My hands are shaking.) 'That's where I want to go now, towards the unknown.'

Later that winter, we go back to Mayto. It is windy, the waves are high and rough; no surfers have ventured out. The beach is deserted except for a few children throwing sticks for dogs. Here, on the other side of the world, I walk by Matilda's side. The years have hollowed out my face, leaving lines around my eyes and on my forehead. The sun has darkened my skin. My hair is going white. Sometimes Matilda strokes it in the evening. She looks at me and smiles. That's as far as we go; it's as good a way of making love as any. We have plenty of time. There's no rush now. I know that she will be the last woman for me.

In front of us, Arginaldo is kicking a football about. He's a teenager now. Sometimes a gust of wind carries the ball far ahead and Arginaldo runs after it, laughing, the way Léon used to laugh when he tried to catch pigeons. Those damn birds; they'd always let him get close but then they'd surge ahead when his little arms were outstretched. After the tenth attempt my son would turn against them, chasing them with pebbles, sticks and kicks.

For a few moments our fingers touch. They don't intertwine. And Matilda smiles the rare smile that lights up her great beauty. We are taking things slowly; wonderfully slowly. Our love doesn't have the ardour of fitting-room encounters. It has the grace of first times, and last times.

It's been more than seven years since I last made love, since I lost myself in the scent of a woman, since I climaxed. There was just the time my finger strayed into my sister's wet mouth, when I was in hospital. They had roughly probed her palate; she had licked them with her tongue, then bitten them with her teeth. She had stifled a cry. My finger had bled. I had wept with pleasure and shame. It's been seven years since anyone made love to me. I feel as if my body has been made anew and the past does not exist.

I have now been living with Matilda and Arginaldo for over a year, in a tiny room costing ten pesos. When I leave the house at dawn, I walk on tiptoe in order not to wake them, stepping cautiously like a *ladrón*, or a heron in a cartoon. We are reunited in the afternoon. I go to meet Arginaldo at the school gates, then we do football practice. Other children have joined us. He can now stop eighty-five balls out of a hundred. His weak spots are still lobs and shots that graze the bar, because he is still small. He wants to grow up fast, but I tell him to take his time, I remind him that childhood is a happy time, a peaceful time. I want to believe in that for him, as I did for Joséphine and Léon, although I know that childhood can also be a desolate place, a wasteland. When you are little, the stars are further away and your dreams are more ambitious. You have to jump to pluck an apple from a tree, to pick some cherries. So many victories are within your grasp.

Here we all sit, facing the ocean. Our shoulders touch. The wind is in our hair, Matilda's locks whip against my cheeks. Her son is holding his football as if it were a precious treasure, a beating heart. His mother stokes his face. He smiles. He doesn't know that she is his mother. He knows nothing of violence or his own history, which is still being written, slowly, cautiously. I am learning things for him that I didn't know for my own children. How to kick a ball. How to lie on the sand and look up at the sky. How to hold hands. The names of different fruits. Matilda looks at me; her dark eyes are soft. Our family is born in silence. In grace. And finally, in peace. The wind has blown in clouds; they are heavy, grey. They hover between the sky and the sea. Arginaldo turns to me.

Why does it rain, Antonio?

Time has passed. And so the time has come.[*]

[*] Clémence Boulouque, *Je n'emporte rien du monde*.

Part Three

23/02

I can't even scream. If I could, I'd scream bad words. Bastard. Fuckwit. I wake up in pain. The pain is horrible. But an evil that doesn't achieve anything. It's been two months, you dog. I like the word *dog*. A dog smells bad, even the word stinks. It's difficult to find the right word for the father who wanted to kill me.

18/04

I managed to say *ah-lo* this morning. Not bad for an eleven-year-old. LOL. Geneviève clapped. She's in charge of my rehabilitation at the hospital. Before she came along, even just saying *o* or *a* made me cry. She's teaching me to talk again, because when I try to say words they slip away, they fall into my scar like they're falling down a crack. When I came here she told me that part of my jaw was gone. I drew a mirror. She said no. It's too soon, Joséphine. My face must have looked horrible. So I wrote *kill me* in my notebook. Kill me! I added at least thirty exclamation marks so that the nurses would be sure to understand. I don't think the nurses can read.

5/05

I watched a film with Geneviève. *The Diving Bell and the Butterfly*, starring Mathieu Amalric. It's the true story of a man who's locked in himself. He can't move his body any more, he can't communicate. All he can do is move his eyelids. And he writes a whole book, letter by letter, just by blinking. A nurse shows him the letters. One blink means yes, two blinks means no. It made me think that actually I've been lucky. In spite of that Dog Shit.

The doctor (the one I don't like) came by. He took the bandages off my monster head. A nurse sprayed my face to get the gauze unstuck. He looked pleased with the graft. They've already done the bone transplant, now it's skin cut from my bottom. It's going to feel like having a bit of ham on my cheek. I wrote in my notebook: horrible? He gave me a stupid smile. It's taking well, I'm pleased. In time it will all be fine, he said, you'll hardly notice a thing. It's a shame I can't laugh. If grown-ups can shoot a girl in the head, then surely it's no big deal to lie to them?

It was Geneviève's idea for me to write things down. She said that pain is like a foreign body. You surround yourself with a kind of shell so you don't feel it. But then you can't recover from something you can't feel.

I haven't written everything down, but don't worry. I'll fill in the gaps.

*

Of course, Léon went off the rails. Léon, Mister WTB (Wets The Bed). His teenage debut. You missed all that. But before that, in the first year of the Dog, when I spent a long time in hospital, he came to see me every day after school. He fed me because sometimes my hands were shaky. He cried as he wiped up the soup running down my chin. Did I burn you? he'd ask, all panicky. But I couldn't feel a thing. My skin was cold. It felt dead, and I imagine it was. Then Léon would climb up on my bed and sit down beside me. He'd lay my head on his shoulder and kiss it to warm it up. We both felt ashamed. We never talked about you. One day he told me he was going to kill you, and that made me happy. My nine-year-old assassin. He brought me books and read them to me. I still remember the words that he stumbled over, as if they were stones: hastened, thundering, yearning. But I only realised later that his biggest struggle was with words of love, those words that hurt because they render you more fragile.

He told me about the outside world. He told me about home, Mama, the Olive. He was trying to grow up quickly. He wanted to be an assassin with a steady hand. He wanted to take judo lessons. Then he could defend himself and protect me. Sometimes he'd comb my hair and that made him proud. One day I asked him to do my eye make-up, but he didn't dare. I'm not going to make it even worse by poking your eye out! Things were good between us. He had dreams for us both. When you're grown up, if you don't have a fiancé I'll stay with you and we'll live together. Then evening would come and a nurse would come in saying it was time for him to leave. One night Léon hid in the toilets down the corridor and then he lay down on the bed with me and we cried. Of course, a nurse found us when she was doing the rounds. She looked at us for a while and then, in the shadows, in the metallic silence of the machines, she told us we looked like angels. Léon said no, angels are dead children, and Joséphine is alive, my sister is stronger than a bullet.

Several months later, when I was back home, we were invited to a fancy dress party. Léon said to me, laughing, you don't need to dress up with a face like yours. And I knew the kind, carefree years of our child-hood were over.

That summer, the Olive went to stay with some friends in Lubéron. One couple had three children; the youngest, at eleven, was only a year older than Léon. So Léon went too. I was jealous, just a little. The Olive had shown us photos, the house had a huge swimming pool, a tennis court, a sauna, a million olive trees, and a river where they could go fishing and canoeing. I think the house belonged to the former head of an advertising agency. Anyway, I stayed at home in Lyon with Mama. She'd try to get back from work early so we could have some 'girls' time'. But she usually spent the evening on the phone. Sometimes she'd take it into her bedroom. I may have been disfigured, but I wasn't deaf; I could hear her words, the syllables, the cutting things she said. They made me sad. I thought of the Mangy Dog. He must have suffered the same scratches. Maybe that was why he had turned into the Human Shit. I decided to talk to the shrink about it. One evening Mama came out of her bedroom with the phone in her hand and beads of sweat on her upper lip. When I was older I understood what it was: pleasure and guilt. We ate melon. Mama said there was no point smelling melons in the shop; melons smelled of melon, and to know if one was ripe you just had to press the little stalk. If it came away easily the melon was ripe. She taught me things :-). In hospital, Geneviève had told me to roll pieces of melon around in my mouth, like when you're trying to make your mouth water, she said it was a good exercise in laterality. I asked her, blushing, whether exercises in laterality would come in useful for kissing a boy some day. She smiled. Will you teach me? Yes, when you can crunch a nut, Joséphine, but not just yet.

After the melon we watched a silly film, but Mama spent most of the time looking at her nails and drinking rosé wine. We didn't really talk. It was more of an idiots' night in than a girls' night in. I told her that she shouldn't feel she was obliged to get home early. Then she took my hands in hers. For a split second I thought I really existed and she was going to talk to me. But then she just began to cry.

On 5 May in the first year of the Dog, the HQ (Horrible Question) came back. Why did you decide to shoot me first?

21/05

That afternoon I came home in an ambulance. A manky
old one, not like the swanky one that took me back
from Paris that night, with spinning lights like flashes of
lightning. Mama and the Olive had hung a banner over
the front door of the apartment. *Welcome Home, Princess.*
The Olive ruffled my hair, then left. Léon was at school.
I put the nurses' presents away in my room. I unpacked
my suitcase with Mama, and then she gave me a present. A big orange scarf. I knew perfectly well why. I
hated them both, her and the scarf.

24/05

It was good at the shrink's today. He's an old man who

smells a bit of dog, but a *nice* dog. He has eyes like a cocker spaniel, there's a sad look in them, with little bits of sleep in the corners. He upsets me sometimes when he looks at me. Because I must be upsetting him, too, with these slices of bacon on my cheek. We worked on words that could explain things, explain the inexpressible (word number one that he taught me). Madness. Depression. Grief. Immense grief. Illness. But I thought those words were too ordinary. What he did to me, what he was about to do to my little brother and then to himself, has no name, according to the doctor. He should have started with himself. I wondered whether you can give a name to something that doesn't exist. The shrink thought that was an interesting thing to say. He advocated (new word number two) carrying on with my search for one. A word is a key, he said, and we are going to need keys.

When I woke up in hospital I was sad. My head felt like it was on fire. Mama was crying, her eyes were all red, the doctors *advocated* getting her to leave the room. Everything was fuzzy. My head hurt so much. Someone asked me what had happened. I didn't know. I was asleep, that's all, and when I woke up it felt as if half of my face was missing. It was like having air where my mouth used to be. I couldn't talk. There was so much blood, the sheets were soaked in it, they were sticking to me. I got up and I saw the Dog leaning over Léon, with a gun. That's all.

The anger didn't come until later.

28/06

Cool! I managed to swallow some cottage pie. I'm sick of soup, ice cream, juice, all the stuff they give old people who are mega-sick and don't have any teeth, like my grandfather. I still have trouble swallowing. Sometimes I dream of eating a steak, or even just a cheese and ham crêpe. The cottage pie was good. The Olive made it. He's done the cooking ever since we moved to Lyon, Madame doesn't have time for that because she has an important job. He works freelance these days. His tattoo collection is growing; he's covered in them. Japanese characters. Yesterday he showed me a new one on his shoulder, *moduru*, which means going back, retracing your steps. He told me it was so he didn't forget that we have never fully settled our scores with the past. I think he smokes too many joints, but sometimes he's cool. These days it's Mama who isn't cool.

It was the first summer in the year of the Dog. I was shut up at home. A piece of meat on my neck hadn't taken well. A reject. Quasimodo was a supermodel compared to me. They gave me cortisone and I started to swell up. I pierced holes in the eyes of the models in my mother's magazines, I blackened their teeth with a biro, I slashed their cheeks. You've no idea how much I hated them. My hand was your hand, the hand that destroyed everything. Outside, in the park just down from our apartment, girls were lying on the grass. They were smoking. They were going out with boys. They were laughing. They were all beautiful. I was twelve and a half and I was a disfigured old hag who would never get better. I'd told the shrink I wanted to kill the Dog, I wanted to hurt you because you had failed. You had failed to kill me, and now my life was a wreck. The shrink wrote down what I said in his notebook, and that made me feel important. But what use was that? It would be the holidays in a month. I wouldn't be able to sit in the sun. I wouldn't be able to go swimming. I wouldn't be able to go out with boys. And my pretty friends already had ugly friends who made them look better. It was the end of a shit childhood, and a shitty start to the next phase of my life. I was growing up deformed. One night I had to be rushed to the burns unit. I had a suppurating mouth. I'll spare you the details.

But this time it had been all right. The graft had been successful. My bottom was striped like a zebra from all the skin they'd taken.

I met Geneviève at the hospital three times a week. I was still talking very slowly, but I was beginning to get through whole sentences without making mistakes. You're making progress, Léon told me one day, his voice very serious. The look on his face made me want to laugh. Laugh. I hadn't laughed in so long, hadn't felt that dizzying feeling; back then I was too scared to laugh. Scared of my jaw dropping open like you see in cartoons. Except that the wolf's jaw would drop whenever a beautiful girl walked by. A beautiful girl, not a girl like me. I was the Elephant Woman.

You see the damage you did.

The shrink went on holiday. It felt funny, being

without him. It felt cold. I wrote down more words: Executioner. Subhuman. HS (Human Shit). Dog Shit. I always came back to the Dog.

One evening, when I was about six or seven, he'd made me laugh. Mama wasn't there and the three of us were having dinner on our own, eating spaghetti and ham. He hadn't cut up the ham very well, and there was a piece I couldn't stuff into my mouth in one go, so it was hanging from my lips, all pink, about ten centimetres long. Papa had looked at me and said: Put your tongue back in, Joséphine. It took me a few seconds to understand, and then I burst out laughing. That had been a good evening.

14/08

Aunt Anna came to visit us today. She lives in Lille. She spent the day with me. It was super. She only says every second word and I talk at a snail's pace – so in the end, we understand each other very well. She told me about the Dog when they were little. How he used to protect her. And the day they'd wanted to go and visit their mother in Bagnolet. My grandmother. She told me about her; it's a very sad story. She's dead now, she died in poverty. But I think the main reason she died was not enough love. Aunt Anna showed me a photo of her. She must have been very beautiful, back in the day. Of course, she looked old-fashioned now because of her hairstyle. But the way she held her cigarette made her look so glamorous, like an actress. There are old photos of Catherine Deneuve in a similar pose. I guess she didn't think my grandfather, the one who has cancer now, was glamorous enough, he was no Mastroianni. I found the name Mastroianni difficult to say, and that made us both laugh. I took care to laugh with my mouth shut. I like Aunt Anna. It's a shame she doesn't have any children, because she'd have been a terrific mother. She explains things well (OK, so she takes her time over it), not like my mother. You have to understand Mama; she's always saying that if no one understands her it's because they aren't paying enough attention. Aunt Anna told me that she had been to see him at the prison hospital. Been to see the Human Dog Shit, I mean. But as I didn't ask her any questions, she didn't say anything more about him. In the evening she took me to the Jardin du Rosaire to see the torchlight procession going up to the cathedral; not because she believes in God or anything like that, but just because it's beautiful. Before we went out, I was just about to put on my horrible orange scarf when she put out her hand to stop me. So I went out with my throat bare for the first time. Aunt Anna took my hand. Out in the crowd people looked at me in the normal way; they smiled at me and I smiled back. Smiling doesn't hurt any more. One boy winked at me. OK, so all he could see was my good side. But still.

Today, the 14 of August, was the nicest day I've had since the night of the Dog.

I went out all on my own today, without a scarf, without a dressing on the area. I tried always to have a wall or something like that on my left side, but it turns out that people don't look at you that much anyway. Or, well, yes, they do. Men did sometimes, old men, usually in their forties, because that day I was wearing denim shorts and I have very long legs; too long, my mother says. There's no reason for her to be jealous; she's more of a bombshell than I am. One day she told me how she'd picked up the Dog. I'd like to have seen that. My mother in her bra, with her big tits, him in trousers that were too long for him. But maybe she shouldn't have been such a flirt, not when you know how it all turned out. She told me they were in love, had been in love, but as time went on she realised he wanted a quiet life and she wanted a tempest. I wouldn't call shooting your daughter a quiet life. I'm seeing the shrink again tomorrow. I'm really very glad about that.

He's usually whiter than white, but this time he was all

tanned. Except for the bits between his fingers, they were still pale; it looked super-cute. We talked about words that might describe the monster. I had some new ones. Sadist. Barbarian. ES (Enormous Shit). He asked me to define them all. Barbarian, for example. I said: someone with no morals, someone who doesn't belong in civilization any more. He nodded, encouraging me to go on. And so I went on: someone who is wild, who's reverted to their animal state, the kind of animal that eats their young. Some turtles do that, sea turtles. And sows, too, some sows eat their own piglets. Sow; that's a good word for him. Finding the right words is import-ant. Then we talked about the way I look. He asked me how I saw myself. In three weeks' time I'll be going back to school. He wanted to know how I felt. I described myself, which wasn't easy, because before the Sow I was pretty on both sides of my face. It's different now. And it's hard to find the words when you're talking about yourself. Before, my mother and even the Olive said that I was pretty; that the boys would be fighting over me. They don't say that any more. They say I'm making progress, it's getting better, it's less obvious. Less obvious, my arse. Anyone would think I have a slice of ham on my left cheek, and it goes right down to my neck; there's a hollow in my jaw. It's as if the boxer with the face tattoo, I forget his name, the one in *A Very Bad*

Trip, had whacked me as hard as he could. They say it's getting better, but I don't see what they see. He gave me a mirror. I still look horrible. He asked me to smile, to take a good look at my smile, and tell him what I saw. A smile, I replied. Are you sure? I took another good look, I smiled a little wider until I was grinning like a maniac. Yes, I'm sure. Are you certain that you're not just making a face? So I looked him straight in the eye, which I don't usually do. And I said thank you, thank you, doctor. Because even if half my face did still look disgusting, my smile had come back. It wasn't all crooked like it was at first, it had that cute kind of look you see in old photos of me, a pretty smile, pretty as a blue sky or a clear night. With no Dog.

29/08

I went shopping with Mama today. We found a nice bag for me to put my school stuff in. The Olive gave me a cool fountain pen. I won't use it, no one uses a fountain pen these days, but it was super-nice of him. He's just been asked to do a big freelance gig for the launch of a new car. He's leaving to spend two weeks in Paris, maybe three. I bet he comes back with another tattoo. And maybe a new car, he joked. He wished me good luck for the new term and told me to smile a lot. I'm freaking out. I've hardly done any lessons this year. Only the bit of long-distance learning that I did at the hospital, in the beginning. So I'll be repeating a year, and that's no good. I'm going to a new school. If I don't make any friends there, I don't care. We tried out all sorts of foundation, and one of them really suited me. That made me feel a bit better.

I remember Answer Number One that I thought of as a response to the HQ (Horrible Question). He tossed a coin.

13/09

The school's not bad. I found a seat next to the windows,
which were on my left. The teachers are pretty cool. The
guy who teaches art is super-cute. And of course he has
a super-gorgeous girlfriend who comes to meet him on
a Vespa. She belongs in an advert. I've made a friend.
Her name is Sacha. She hates her name because she once
had a neighbour she didn't like – he wore a silly Ricard
baseball cap – and he called his dog Sacha. It was a Great
Dane the size of a small donkey. I told her I thought
Joséphine was a stupid name, all uptight and bourgeois
and serious. She didn't agree. It's very chic, she said.
Like you. Because of that *like you* we became friends. She
is such a ginger, she has millions of tiny orange freckles
on her face, arms, shoulders and breasts. I like to imagine that if you shook her hard enough, they'd fly off her

and go whirling through the air. That would be a pretty sight. But she thinks her freckles are ugly. Look at my hands, it looks like someone's stuck thousands of rusty nails into them. I became friendly with her because she's similar to me; we don't like ourselves that much, we don't like the way we are. But at the same time, you have to learn to like yourself. That's what the shrink told me. Sacha came home with me today, and we did our home-work in my room, but mostly we listened to *Mardy Bum* on a loop. We made a list of all the boys in our class. There are seven very ugly ones, two who are so-so, one who's a possible, four who are not bad, and one who's really hot. But we don't kid ourselves too much, Sacha with her freckles and me with my slice of ham.

14/09

Patrick Swayze is dead. Why couldn't it have been Mel Gibson instead?

04/10

She asked what happened to me. Of course, I didn't dare tell her the truth. The truth is still too hard. It means saying so many horrible things: being eaten by the Sow, snuffed out by the Human Shit. It means I might also be a Sow, or a piece of Human Shit who doesn't deserve love, or the affection that makes life so good. I told her I'd been in a car crash and wasn't wearing my seat belt, so I'd gone through the windscreen. She made a *sceptical* sort of face.

In two weeks' time it will be autumn half-term. She's invited me to go away with her. Her parents have a holiday home at Uriage-les-Bains, near Grenoble. We'll be going to the spa there. Very chic.

10/10

I got a grade of seventeen for my drawing this morning. We had to do our self-portraits in the style of a famous artist. I chose Francis Bacon.

29/10

This is wild. Sacha's mother gave us the ultimate all-in package at the spa: *Total Relaxation*. For three days. Hydromassage baths. (I love them.) Mud packs (not so sure). Jet showers. A hydrotherapy pool. Solarium.

Turkish bath. Relaxation room. We were the youngest and prettiest there. The older women looked jealous at first, with a hint of scorn in their expression, too. But then they looked at us with sympathy because of our strange faces. Sacha's rusty nails. My charcuterie.

Sacha's mother is brilliant. We talk for ages, sometimes late into the night. I feel like a grown-up around her; that I'm important and that I exist just as I am. I'd like to be able to tell her what happened to me one day. Without fear or shame. Because I'm beginning to suspect that at some point, behind all the horror, beyond the terror, there was love.

21/11

Answer Number Two to the HQ. He was afraid that if he shot Léon first, the noise would wake me. I'd see him doing it. And I wouldn't love him any more.

Filling in the gaps (continued).

*

On my fifteenth birthday, Léon was suspended from school for three days. The Olive went to pick him up. They walked in the park for a long time. I could see them from my window. Léon was shaking his head. At one point he tried to run away, but the Olive caught up with him; the scene looked like a father telling off his son. The Olive was shouting and waving his arms about. I don't remember you ever telling us off. Shouting at us. Or hitting us. You liked a quiet life, as Mama used to say; you were reserved. An introvert. Ah, there's a nice long word, he's *introverted*. I talked about that to the shrink, internalization: refusing to let your emotions out, the fear of losing control. Because after what you did to me, my anger took some time to come out. At first I felt ashamed. I felt I was a Piece of Shit. When your father doesn't want you any more, it has to be your fault. That's what I thought for a long time: I didn't make him happy enough, I was a disappointment, I was ugly, I wasn't funny, I wasn't graceful, I wasn't beautiful. My eyes didn't shine like water. Although mine are the same colour as his. Because he was my father, I never thought that he might be the problem. I went on to the internet to try to find girls who'd been through the same thing, but their fathers (and sometimes their mothers) were better shots than mine. I didn't find any other survivors. Instead, I found a lot of cases of incest, violent fathers, pathological liars, those who refused to accept a daughter's pregnancy. But not a single other case of a daughter surviving a father's attempt to end her life.

Writing 'survivor' for the first time is funny. It's a word that I couldn't have imagined using before. The shrink and I talked about it. A survivor: a person who stays alive after an incident in which there were victims, says the dictionary.

I stayed alive.

But not knowing why is what's difficult.

On my fifteenth birthday Léon was suspended for punching another boy in the face. As they were coming out of school, the boy had said, 'Your dad's a pervert.' And that evening, when I told my brother that our father was much worse than that, he shook his head. He's not my real father, Léon said. The other one is.

Later the Olive bought a motorbike. A big Triumph. It made one hell of a noise. Girls turned in the street to look at it, and so did men. The Olive took Léon to school on it, and Léon felt like Batman. When they parted they bumped fists, like two gangsters. Léon wanted a tattoo for Christmas. He had already chosen his symbol. 不羈独立. He had enlarged it and stuck it to his bedroom wall. *Fukidokuritsu*. Free and independent. Mama rolled her eyes. In your dreams, my poor child, no one gets tattoos when they're twelve. I'm nearly thirteen, Léon replied. He gave her an evil look. I could see clearly what he didn't dare say to her face: Shut up, I'll do what I want. Mister Two-Faced Bastard. I thought he hated Mama because of you. We never talked about it again. Not ever. After I came out of hospital, Léon and I decided we wanted to change our surname, we didn't want to be Joséphine Sow, or Léon Sow.

We had burned all the photos of that monstrous Sow. We had broken all the things the Sow had ever given us, had even touched. We wanted to wipe it out.

Kill it. We never said *Papa*. We never mentioned you. Sometimes, if you don't talk about things they cease to exist.

But I have to talk about it now if I want to exist.

Mama and the Olive were fighting more and more. Because of the motorbike. Because he was coming home later and later. Because his jacket sometimes smelled of perfume, or his hair of smoke. He replied *she could talk*. If you see what I mean, he added with a nasty smile. One day he went as far as to say: We all know about you and your changing rooms. That time she slapped him then went into her bedroom and slammed the door. Léon ran over to the Olive to hug him. The Olive ruffled his hair. Get your helmet, my biker comrade, he said, and off they went.

That day Léon got a tattoo. *Fukidokuritsu*. On his shoulder, level with the deltoid muscle. He showed it to me, making me promise not to tell Mama. Or I'll kill you. You wouldn't be the first one to try, I replied, and it won't work, I'm immortal, don't you know? I rather liked that idea – of being immortal. I'd discussed it with the shrink. The Dog had tried to shoot a hole in me. Of course, I was going to die one day, like everyone else, but not this time. If I was a survivor, if I was alive, maybe that was because I had something worth living for. A life of my own, a story of my own, surrounded by people I would have chosen. People I would love, and who would love me, even with my ham face. And my nice smile, my heartbreaker smile. I know that Mama's relationship with the Olive was nothing to write home about. I'd talked about it to Sacha and her mother one night. We talked about desire. All those things, those incandescent things (*incandescent* was another new word). The damage desire could do. The loss that often followed. Because no one can exist in a permanent state of desire. It's too fraught, it consumes itself. Sacha said she would never marry, she'd only have lovers. Her mother laughed. All I said was that my one real desire was to start my periods. I was fifteen and I still hadn't started, because someone had dried up my heart and drained all the blood away. A Vampire Dog.

25/12

Christmas. Huh. The Olive and Mama tried to be nice. Aunt Anna and Uncle Thomas came from Lille by train. I got some shoes from Zadig & Voltaire. A bottle of perfume, Daisy by Marc Jacobs. A voucher from H&M for three hundred euros. An Amy Winehouse CD (I already had it, but thanks, Mama). A bareMinerals kit. And a beautiful old watch (that still works), a Reverso. The initials inside are nothing like mine. I didn't even look at Léon's presents. I couldn't have cared less. We hadn't spoken since he threatened to kill me. I still called him Mr WTB. Wets The Bed. It really upset him, which pleased me. Aunt Anna told me the latest news about my grandpa. She said they were waiting. Well, she said *we're* and her husband said *waiting*. Uncle Thomas is the only person who really understands what she is saying, along with the HS, and me just a bit. It could be tomorrow, in a year's time, in two years' time. They're waiting. And she said that Colette looks more and more like someone suffering from Parkinson's. But it wasn't Parkinson's, it was her fear of being abandoned, of finding herself alone one morning, that was making her shake. It was terrible, because when she was feeding my grandfather she spilt food everywhere, then she'd apologise, she felt so ashamed, she'd cried such a lot because of that.

So Aunt Anna paid a lady whose hands wouldn't tremble to come at mealtimes, and make small talk with them: about the roadworks in the Rue de Belfort, the death of the hairdresser from the Rue des Chaudronniers, a dog that had been run over. She gave me a present from Colette. A little ring. A *teeny-weeny* diamond. A link between us. Even if she was married to the Monster's father, I like that link, the idea of having a family. Of not being entirely alone, rejected, murdered. The grown-ups stayed in the sitting room. I went to my bedroom to write this and then I called Sacha.

8/01

This morning Mama talked about sending Léon to a boarding school, and the Olive didn't agree. She said:

I'm his mother. And Léon said: The Olive is my father. In fact, he yelled it. Mama put her hand to her mouth, as if she was trying to stop herself from screaming or throwing up. She suddenly looked very sad. I said that boarding school would do Mr WTB some good, he'd be less of a smart-arse. The Olive told me to shut up.

I hate them all. I hate them all. I hate them all.

8/01 (Night)

Answer Number Three to the HQ. He was afraid of girls.

21/01

The shrink and I played a game today. He asked me to describe the kind of person I'd like to be when I grow up. I didn't know what to say. He waited.

Then I said: Normal. And he said: But you already are normal. I said no. Normal is when other people love you.

At the end of spring, Mama discovered the tattoo on Mr WTB's shoulder. She went spare. She told the Olive to leave. Get out of the house. She said he was irresponsible, she was going to call the police. Letting a child get a tattoo! The Olive went off on his motorbike and Léon stopped doing any work at school. He was spiteful, nasty. Sometimes Mama cried at night. Sometimes she didn't sleep at home – like before, during the time of the Sow. She would come back in the morning with croissants, as if to say: 'See what a good mother I am?' But I saw her red eyes, her dirty skin, greasy because she hadn't taken off her make-up. The tangles in her hair, the scratches on her neck and hands. In her heart. I could tell that she was suffering. And I told the shrink that the HS ought to have seen that too. You can't escape other people's suffering, it hits you in the face. It needs you. In spite of you. We talked a lot about that. Suffering, grief, injuries, torments. We drew up a scale of one to ten and I tried to place things on that scale.

The ham on my cheek was getting lighter, it was beginning to look like a birthmark. You can live with a birthmark. The hole in my jaw was still there. I chewed gum. I smoked. I was compensating. I smiled a lot. A hairdresser gave me a great cut and it was like the thing with the Dog Shit had never happened. Sometimes a boy would ask me to Starbucks after school, not the hottest guy in the class, not one of the 'not bad' guys, but not one of the ugliest either. OK, Joséphine, could do better.

I was still seeing Geneviève twice a week and my elocution, four years on, had become 'eloquent', as she said. I knew I'd never be an actress or a TV presenter (and that was no bad thing), but I loved Geneviève's encouragement. No, my real suffering was on the inside. It was huge, an abyss, it gnawed away at my stomach my heart my bones. I couldn't take it any more. If it didn't disappear, then I would have to.

Of course, I thought about it. You know what? Let me finish off your dirty work. I was even thinking about different approaches. A gentle approach, like an overdose; or a drastic one. I'd go for the drastic, violent one. Joséphine, the daughter of a monster. Can't be put back together again. Our flat was on the seventh floor.

A twenty-one-metre drop. For 2.068 seconds, I would fly. I would hit the ground at 73.1 kilometres per hour. Imagine how my face would look on the pavement, as if a 0.8 kilo bowling ball had just smashed into it. Better than your stupid bullet. I'd be mush. Irreparable.

You didn't know that I was good at physics.

When I told him all this, the shrink said: In a way you are like *him*. You're drawn to extremes. You're passionate. I jumped up and marched out of his shitty study and slammed the door. It was raining. And I realised I had never asked him, never asked my father why it rains.

Sacha has been going out with a boy. He's in his final year at school. He's no Camille Lacourt, she said, but I'm no Valérie Bègue. He was eighteen, and a bit of a goth. Quiet during the week, weird at weekends: he wore steampunk glasses and had an industrial vibe, which went well with her rusty-nail freckles. We laughed at that like banshees. They lasted a month. Well, twenty-six days to be precise. She dumped him, partly because he wanted to sleep with her, but mainly because he was depressing. He was a good enough kisser, though. He had a very long tongue, he could touch his chin with it. But it was gross when he did that, it looked like a limp dick. How I laughed about it with Sacha. I love her. She's my sister. I told her about the Human Shit. And what he did to me. We cried. I felt good.

And then the Olive came back. My mother had

asked him to. I think Léon and I frightened her, the two children of the HS. She didn't really want to be a mother enough to be left on her own with us. She liked the stuff she did in department-store changing rooms. Seduction, conquest. I thought my mother was very beautiful. What made her even more beautiful was that she was dangerous. I'd have liked to be more like her, but at the same time I wouldn't. There is a calm place inside me that I'm happy with. I know, Mr Shrink, I know. Calm. Like *him*. I get it from *him*. It brings me closer to *him*.

When the Olive came back Léon became a nice little brother again. He did his homework. He washed (because sometimes he really stank). He brushed his teeth, sometimes he put on deodorant, he flushed the loo. He even told me I wasn't bad-looking. I was no Eva Mendes, no Selma Hayek, but still, not bad-looking. Life at home was a dream. LOL. My mother and the Olive kissed on the mouth when we were around. He put his hand on her bottom, and she wriggled, laughing; they played at being in love, at desire. Once he took her out on the motorbike and she came home all hysterical, talking like a porn star. Léon began to cry and the Olive told him: Don't worry, mate, I only have one biker comrade and that's you. And off they went down the Fourvière tunnel.

Otherwise, it was cool at school. I was getting very good grades, I'd go up to next year's class with Sacha. And finally it happened. My period started.

19/09

I went out with a boy that summer. But I didn't let him kiss me. Even though, with all the stuff Geneviève had taught me, I should have been the Queen of Kissing. We talked so much about girl things. I adored her. I let the boy feel me up, put one finger in me, two. But I wouldn't let him go near my mouth. I talked to the shrink about that. Very Freudian, he said, amused. I told him my mouth was a sanctuary. The tabernacle of my pain, the place of my death, the scar of my rebirth. I had become a little serious, I know.

I ask myself a lot of questions. Right now I'm full of *whys*. Why do we never talk about him, Mama, why did he do that, why did the two of you have children if you didn't love each other? Why me? Why does desire always begin in fire and end in ashes? I wonder why I cry like this for no reason. Why I'm ashamed. Why I can feel all this wind and cold inside me.

Clément. That was the boy's name. He was nice. A little clumsy with his fingers. *Butterfingers*, Sacha called him. And we burst out laughing. Clément wasn't very bright. All the same, he was nice. He didn't make a fuss. He didn't say silly words about love. He said words like vagina, penis, breasts, exploring each other. And then he went to stay with his grandma in an old farmhouse at Ristolas, five kilometres from Aiguilles. A little village in the Alps. There were animals, he told me, cows and goats. The hands that had felt me up for two weeks were going to milk them. I was glad I hadn't kissed him. Kissing is too serious. But the idea of being like a cow in a man's hands disgusted me.

20/09

My mother and the Olive have gone off for a week on their own. I've no intention of looking after Mr WTB (he's started shaving to try and make his moustache grow), cooking for him, cleaning up after him, checking his school bag in the morning. Or helping with his homework in the evening. I'm not his maid or his mother. That's not very cool, the Olive said. And I'm not his father either, I added. It was all rather tense. They were going away to give themselves another chance, which made me laugh: giving themselves a chance. The shrink asked me why it made me laugh. Because that's just an illusion if they haven't said sorry to each other. A chance is the gift of forgiveness. So then we talked about forgiveness, and that's really hard because it brings up such weighty questions. Weighty enough to crush you. I have a feeling that the gunshot will go on for ever, and the noise of it will never stop. There are some words that make me feel physically ill when I try to say them. Like sorry.

Forgiving. Caressing. Childhood. Affection. Acceptance. Papa.

24 / 10

Answers Numbers Four, Five and Six to the HQ. Because he changed his mind at the last minute and wanted to keep Léon with him. Because he thought that I'd lived longer than my brother, so my brother deserved more time. Because he loved me too much.

25/10

We skipped school today because it was Sacha's birthday. I gave her a very nice coat from Zara. It was red with black buttons, cut in a fifties, Hepburn style. Sacha sets everything alight with her fiery hair. People whistled at us in the street. Guys. Married men. Men gagging for it. That made us laugh. In Starbucks, an old guy wanted to pay for our coffees and blueberry muffins. We turned him down and he turned on us as if we were little bitches. Men are far from being cured yet, if you ask me. Then we went to see *The Paperboy*, with Zac Ephron, Matthew McConaughey, and Nicole Kidman (very hot). The scene in prison where she touches herself up isn't bad. The ending is very violent. We ate two tons of popcorn, laughing like crazy every time McConaughey showed off his abs (though I took good care not to dislocate my jaw). When we came out of the cinema the weather was lovely. We walked along the Saône, down the Quai Joseph-Gillet and the Quai Saint-Vincent. It was an amazing day. Just Sacha and me. Rusty nails and a slice of ham. Outside time. We were floating on air.

When I was tidying up my things yesterday evening, I found that letter a journalist wrote me two years ago. She had wanted to meet me so she could write a book about what happened. The very idea got me down. Lana Del Rey all over. 'Blue Jeans' in a loop.

I hope remorse kills.

*

Of course, I went back to hospital regularly. Examinations, X-rays, tests. Everyone was very pleased. I asked about the slice of ham. They didn't understand me at first. There was no place for humour in the horror of it all. They tried to reassure me. There'll always be a small mark, Joséphine. But in time the pigmentation will come close to the colour of the rest of your skin. In time I'd look really good. Yeah, right.

Geneviève taught me to sing. I did exercises. It was horrible. My voice was shocking. You destroyed that, too. She showed me how to find singers on YouTube, which wasn't so much fun. I made her listen to 'Acceptable in the 80s' and 'Bad Romance'. She invited me to the hospital canteen. It felt funny, tasting things I'd eaten every day for six months. Tasting the disgust I felt for you. With the shrink, I retraced my steps, all that grief. One day, in his consulting room, I looked at myself in the mirror for a long time. Admit it, he said, admit you're still pretty. I did understand: Yes, I'm still pretty. He sighed. You're growing up at last! I smiled. On my left cheek, the horrible one, my little dimple was very slowly coming back, finding its place. I was very pleased. And there were my eyes as well, eyes as green as water, like the Dog Shit's eyes. And, I think, like the eyes of my grandfather who let my grandmother die a loveless death. People always looked at my eyes. I was lucky to have a good figure. Thanks, Mama. My legs are longer than hers. My legs make people go wild, Sacha used to say (she still does). I decided to stop complaining about my face. I felt good when I left the shrink's office that day.

But that night my mum and the Olive had a big row. If they split up, Léon said, he'd live with the Olive. His biker comrade. My mother went nuts when he said that, she shouted things like: You'll do as I tell you, I'm your mother, I make the decisions. When Mr WTB, Mr Beardless, talked back – To hell with that, I'll run away, I'll get myself out of here – my mother flung a vase against the wall. Shards of broken glass flew through the air and some of them hit Léon's face. He was bleeding in two places. When he touched his cheek, his palm came away red, like when you paint with your hand. I fainted.

The shame of it, a little later. Léon was furious. You pissed yourself! You pissed yourself! He was wearing two little plasters, one on his forehead, one on his cheek. Nothing serious. The emergency doctor gave me something to help me sleep. The world suddenly went soft. The mattress, the duvet. I was a stone wrapped in cotton wool. I heard the Sow's voice. Far, far away. Yes, your voice. It was reading *Hansel and Gretel*. I fell into a deep sleep.

In those last sessions with the shrink we talked about memories a lot. About the time before Léon came along. I remembered it very well. My mother and I got his room ready. She had an enormous belly and her breasts were huge. There was even a photo of her displaying her breasts. We bought him cuddly toys. She let me choose them. I did all these drawings for his room and we hung them from tacks using coloured thread. My mother had planted pink and purple flowers in our garden. The HS took photos of us. He said we were beautiful, we made him happy; he thanked us.

So?

So I don't want to admit it, but that was a very good time in my life. My parents were getting on well. Getting on well again, I mean. I was in the middle of them. I loved them both. We should have had a nice life ahead of us. And then that.

What?

You know perfectly well.

He wanted me to be the one who said it. This was Therapy, of course, Therapy with a capital T. The words have to come out. You have to spit them out if you want to get better. So I talked. I talked about the day just before the night of the Dog.

2 / 12 (at night, everyone is asleep)

Some days are perfect. There's no reason to distrust them, you think they're normal. As soon as I got up I felt something different in the air. First the light outside. The sky was very blue and everything was sharply defined, like in a photograph. The air seemed clean, if you see what I mean. He had gone to buy croissants and milk rolls. The milk rolls were for Léon, who loves to eat them with Nutella. The three of us had breakfast together. We laughed. We talked about what we wanted to do that day. He said: whatever you want. Léon and I didn't want much. I mean, we didn't want to go to the museum or to Noëtica. We just wanted to enjoy the day together. Stay at home, put on some music. Dance. And that's what we did. I'd never seen him dance. He looked funny. I taught him some rock 'n' roll, but he didn't have any rhythm. Then, since we were in swimsuits, he showered us with the garden hose, even though the water was cold. Léon and I said it would be great to have a swimming pool one day, and he said, Right, OK, we'll get a pool. A real one, asked Léon, not some shitty plastic thing? A real one. With a diving board. And warm water, said Léon. We laughed. We laid out string to mark the sides of the pool and he promised he'd call someone the following day. In three months, when spring came, we could all go swimming. That was how we spent the day. Doing family stuff. Dreaming little dreams. After that we made lunch together. I made a salad, I'm good at salads. Léon laid the table. He opened a bottle of wine. He gave us a little and we drank to the swimming pool. To the blue sky. To our grandfather's health, to his cancer going away. To Colette, so she'd stop shaking. To Mama, so she'd come back one day. He asked us to forgive him for all the times he hadn't been a great father. Léon got up and gave him a hug, saying that he *had* been a great father.

Answer Number Seven to the HQ. Because I didn't tell him he was great.

He was really moved by Léon's hug. He rubbed his eyes. He told us that he loved us, that he would get another job soon and everything would be all right. We had a delicious lunch – I have to say my salad went down very well. Léon asked if he could go to judo classes. He didn't sound very keen on that, but he said yes anyway, and Léon immediately got up to do his stupid moves, trying to be his hero, Jason Bourne. I talked to him about school, and what I'd like to do when I grew up. I wanted to be a fashion designer or a perfumier. I'd read a book by the man who made almost all the Hermès perfumes and I'd loved it. I liked the language in the book, these words that had a smell, these phrases that were so silent and so precise they left a trace behind. He listened to me for a long time and I felt good. Grown-up. Proud, because he was spending so much time with me. Léon was watching a video. He and I were still sitting at the table. He asked me to describe the kind of perfume I would make. It was a difficult question. Nougat. Malabar chewing gum. A touch of liquorice. A little hyacinth. (Mama had planted hyacinths in our garden.) With bits of childhood too, I said. He thought that sounded good. He closed his eyes, as if he could smell the perfume I had just invented. He stroked my cheek. He smiled at me. You will always keep your wonderful bits of childhood, Joséphine, believe me. And I believed him. In that instant there was nothing I wanted more than to believe my Papa. I know I did. That, said the shrink, is the first time you've said 'my Papa' since we've known each other.

My Papa. Suddenly those are strange words, burning my mouth, piercing my skin like needles. But they are also warm, comfortable words.

We washed the dishes together and he took us to the Montois bakery for dessert. He explained why the Negroes' Heads had become Othello cakes, but – he added – you don't make people kinder just by changing the name of a cake. You don't make them kinder or more generous. He told us that the job-centre interviews were tough; cruel things were said and they hurt. He told us that one woman had collapsed when she was told she was losing her benefits. They said she had no right to anything. Those were dreadful words to say: no right to anything. He talked to us as if we were adults. Léon and I felt important. It was great. We asked him lots of questions and he answered them. At one point he said that there was a question we had never asked him, and he wished we had. What question, Papa? Why does it rain? And Léon said: Because the weather forecast says so, Papa. We laughed. But I saw a sad look in my father's eyes. When we got home we played Monopoly; it was a crazy game. I was losing. He was the banker, so he slipped me five-hundred-euro notes under the table. We were terrified that Léon would see us. That afternoon, the greenish-yellow notes passed under the table were our secret. Our last great secret.

In the evening, we had pizza. We watched *Die Hard 1* for Léon, though he'd seen it a hundred times. Then *LOL* for me, though I'd seen it a thousand times. All three of us sat on the sofa. We ate M&Ms. Afterwards, he told us to go to the bathroom and brush our teeth well. The teeth you have now are important, he said, because you won't be able to grow them again. Wash your face, your hands, behind your ears. Pay attention, because I'm going to check when you're in bed. We shouted and laughed. That day, we had been grown-ups and we had been children. We had had our father all to ourselves. We were going to have a swimming pool in the garden. He was going to get a new job. Maybe our grandfather's cancer would go away. It was the best day of our lives. We'd had another best day of our lives, but that was before Mama left. This was the best day of our lives with Papa. Shit, I've written it down. But it's true; that day he was the best Papa in the world. He read *Hansel and Gretel* to us in bed. It was the story he always used to read to Aunt Anna when they were little, and Aunt Anna, with the covers up to her nose would whisper: *Speak quietly, scared loud*. She meant: Speak more quietly, I'm scared of loud words.

We had hugs. Lots of hugs. Then he repeated that he

loved us, that he loved us more than anything, but it was time to go to sleep, there'd be school tomorrow and it would be a big day.

Night fell.

19/05

Sacha and I are moving up to the next class. High five. Average grades of 16.2 (Sacha) and 15.8 (me). Ham and rusty nails are taking their revenge. We're the strongest. We're the prettiest. Our mothers are hysterical. They're going to take us shopping. *Non-stop shopping, girls!*

OK, it's not as great as it sounds. Non-stop means anything up to four hundred euros. But still . . .

And then they came to tell my mother that you had been released. For a few seconds she was frozen stiff. They had to make her sit down and reassure her. He won't be coming here, Madame, he isn't asking for anything. Not even to see us? Don't worry. They were gentle with her. A woman gave her a pill. This will relax you. Then we have nothing to fear? asked my mother. Nothing. He said he was going away, and you would never hear from him again. He asked that you would forgive him, but he knows that you will not. So he's as good as dead, said my mother. And Léon showed off, saying that if you came back he'd kill you, and the Olive added, I'll help you, my biker comrade. They bumped fists.

On that day, three years after the night of the Dog, on Monday, 7 June 2010, there was no pain in my jaw. I did not stammer. I was not sad. I said, *Papa has gone* the same way I'd say, *The storm is over, the fire has gone out*, or *The meal is ready, we can sit down to eat*.

It was as if a thousand tons of toxic fumes and blood had suddenly fallen away from my shoulders, from my hips, slid down my too-long legs. And I let my period flow, warm and sticky. My mother came over and took me in her arms. She was trembling. The blood dripped onto her feet before the living-room carpet soaked it up. She was crying. I was smiling. My dimple was smiling. I felt light. Cleansed. Alive.

*

It was as if you were dead.

21/05

This morning, I turned seventeen. This morning, my grandfather died. What a present, Sacha said. I'm going to Lille straightaway. The direct train takes three hours. You don't have to go, my mother said. But I want to. She's not going, Léon isn't either; he said he couldn't care less. It wasn't his grandfather – he says his real grandfather is the Olive's father, and a murderer's father isn't worth the bother.

22/05

I'm at Aunt Anna's, in a very pretty room overlooking a garden. They have a little house in the old part of Lille. We went to Cambrai early this morning to see Colette.

She was sitting down and had stopped shaking. When my grandfather died, her hands had fallen to her knees like two rotten fruits. She's stopped biting her lips and had pressed them tight together. She held her head at an angle, but it was perfectly still. Within an hour her hair had finished turning white; it looked like a bride's veil. Then it occurred to me that it was my grandfather's life, breathing inside her, that had been making her shake. From now on there was no more of this breath, only resignation. The grief she felt was motionless, and as heavy as a stone. She took me in her limp arms. I stayed there for a long time. Then she told us that the last few weeks had been dreadful, he couldn't even eat bits of a clementine, she'd squeeze them just above his mouth so that the juice ran over his lips and his chin; his tongue hadn't been strong enough to lick it up. He weighed almost nothing. The imponderable weight of regret. When you die, what do you regret not having loved enough? He didn't recognise her any more. His eyes didn't open, but they still shed tears. Was he crying for what my father had done? During those last few weeks Colette's shaking had become worse than ever. It was violent, she moved like a hurricane, as if she were trying to power a dynamo that would maintain the spark of my grandfather's life. Her gesticulations had done a lot of damage to the house. Aunt Anna and I spent the morning doing housework, cleaning up the dirt that accumulates during a slow death, picking up the debris of a life, the mementos. In the mess I found a postcard my father had written in the summer of 1983. He and Aunt Anna had gone to a summer camp in l'Alpe-d'Huez. He had been thirteen. 'I'm sorry I was horrible to you,' he had written to Colette. 'I'll try to make an effort. But don't think that you're my mother, or my sister's mother.' I'd never imagined my father as a thirteen-year-old. I'd never imagined the childhood he'd had, with one sister dead and the other only saying half of what she meant. With an absent mother. And Colette as the target for his anger. Colette, even back then, suffering from her involvement.

Aunt Anna took us all to a restaurant and Uncle Thomas joined us. Colette didn't eat much; she cried a great deal, hiding her face in her napkin. I was upset, because she's so kind. She had been there for Léon, like a Mama. She had come immediately on that dreadful night. When I'd been rushed to hospital, when my mother was sleeping with some guy or other in Paris or Nice, when our lives were turned upside down.

It's late, but I'm going to call Sacha. Because she makes me feel normal.

23/05

I've just passed by our old house. The new people have put flowers in the first-floor window boxes. You won't believe this, Sacha, but they're hyacinths. Memories have blossomed. My father. My mother. All of us. Fragments of my childhood, like jigsaw pieces. You never see what the final picture will look like, but you want to. You grow up just to find out, and you want to grow up fast. I told myself that you never know what happiness is until it's gone; you never know when you're actually living it, contrary to grief. Since I've been here with Aunt Anna, I want happiness for myself. And peace. It's scary. I called the shrink this afternoon to talk about this unexpected need to find my family, my place within it. That's good, he said, you want to live for what you are now, not what you've been through. Finally. What I've been through. His phrase evokes compassion, distress, disgust, scorn. I remember the idiot at school last year who called me Photoshop. I didn't say anything. Stupid remarks don't deserve a reply. They don't deserve anything. I asked Aunt Anna if she knew where my father was. She looked surprised. Why?

So you can tell him his father died.

23/05 (11.20 p.m.)

I wonder if it's going to be sad. I don't know whether I'll feel sad. The funeral is tomorrow.

24/05

The weather was wonderful. Maybe that's why so many people came. So many of them were widows and spinsters, Aunt Anna told me. Customers from Raismes, Jenlain, Saint-Aubert, back when my grandfather was the perfect pharmacist, the apple of those ladies' eyes. Having seen him dead, all wasted away, his innards hoovered out, I find it hard to imagine him being so charming that he made them all sigh. Why was my grandmother so sad that she left him? So sad that she abandoned her children? A few people said nice things about him. Colette was going to read a passage from *The Little Prince*, but she was crying too much and the tears drowned her words. After the funeral there was a reception in the café near the pharmacy where he used to work, and where he liked to go now and then. Kir, 'pain surprise' – a hollowed-out loaf filled with savouries – and macaroons. Funerals made you hungry, the emptiness of them. I recognised several people. Misshapen figures. And suddenly, there was his. It was a shock. He must have put on twenty kilos. FFF. He had been my father's childhood friend, his best friend. He had given us presents and he said he'd always be there for us. Like all adults do, he was lying. I looked at him until our eyes met. He didn't exactly make a beeline for me; he tried to avoid me, and I know why. I went over to him all the same. There was a long, awkward pause. He downed two kirs in quick succession and his wife shot him a nasty look. Then he asked me to forgive him. Me. I'm sorry, Joséphine, forgive me for letting your father down after what he did, for not being a friend to him, a real friend, and for not trying to find out how you were. He said he felt ashamed. Seven years of shame, of misfortune. I was afraid, he said. I feel sick every morning. I shit blood. My fingers are getting so stiff I can't shake hands properly these days. My betrayal is killing me, my sweet; friends should be there for each other through all the anger and madness. Through blood and storms. I miss your bastard father. I miss his cowardice. It was really just a huge, timid love of life. I've been drinking too much since that awful night. The minute I wake up, I think of him, and then I try to drown that thought. I'm slowly poisoning myself. I can't forgive myself, Joséphine, and you have the right to despise me, to spit in my face. I'm not a very good man. In fact, I'm a shit.

His eyes were shining. With emotion, kir, shame. It was a bad mixture.

Yes, you are a shit, FFF, I said, and I spat at him. His wife took his arm and tugged on it, as if she were tugging at a dog's lead. He picked up another glass from a table and raised it to his lips. She knocked it away. The glass broke and the kir spilled, forming a puddle on the floor the colour of blood. FFF looked at me, his eyes lost in the distance, while his wife pushed him outside onto the pavement, where he collapsed. Remorse was eating away at him. It was his own kind of cancer. And I thought: I hope he dies of it.

Only crazy people would wish for the death of another person.

20.20 p.m. Too late to call the shrink.

24/05 (later)

Aunt Anna and I were in the kitchen. Uncle Thomas was asleep, but we couldn't sleep. She opened a bottle of wine, got out some cheese, and we toasted the bread left over from that morning. We talked about so many things. It was a bit slow-going, but we had plenty of time. And I love her. I haven't talked to my mother like that for many years. She doesn't talk to us much at all these days, she's away for her job more and more, sometimes she goes abroad for days on end. The Olive looks after Léon. He's taught him how to ride the motorbike. And even to do wheelies. That's how idiots get into accidents and end up in wheelchairs. They tell me to mind my own business and we always end up having a row. They're both idiots. I can't wait to take my Bac and then clear off. Aunt Anna and I talked about so many things. She has fond memories of her brother. It's hard for me to believe that she's talking about my father. Or that he was ever like that: a really cool brother, always there for her, thoughtful. She told me that one day he bought her lots of Malabar gum thinking that, if she chewed it, the muscles in her mouth would strengthen and then the missing words could come out. When they went to summer camp, he'd insist on staying with her at night because she was afraid. And so he could read her *Hansel and Gretel* without anyone laughing at them. When she met Thomas, the three of them were inseparable. She visited my father at the psychiatric hospital five years ago, after we had gone to live in Lyon. When she told him about my HQ she said he cried. And she told him that Léon and I had destroyed everything that might remind us of him and that we'd even rejected his name. After that he had refused to see anyone, and they hadn't spoken since.

The day was breaking outside and we were yawning. She gave me an envelope for my birthday. It contained the only two things she had left of their mother, my father's and hers.

It's a present that tells you that happiness does exist, Joséphine, it definitely existed somewhere.

There were two photos in the envelope. The first was of two little twins wearing pink dresses; they are pale and beautiful. They are in a garden, laughing. They look immortal. Behind them, hyacinths the colour of their dresses are in bloom. The second photo, taken in a booth, shows a six-year-old boy with neatly combed hair and a white shirt buttoned up to the neck. It was taken for his registration at a judo class, Aunt Anna explained, but then he stopped doing judo. He had told her that the day that photo was taken was the best day of his life.

After the photo was taken, he went to the cinema with their mother, and they had ice-cream cones.

I'm going back tomorrow.

27/08

Sacha and I are in Spain, celebrating having passed our Bac. (Her average was 16.1. Mine was 15.9, damn it.) Sacha has decided to study maths, and I'm going to study chemistry. Like my grandfather. But unlike him, I want my studies to leave their mark on me, I don't want to efface them. I'd like to create perfumes one day.

Some nights we dance till dawn. Sacha goes out with lots of boys. She doesn't mind who. She's always said she would only have lovers. It's more complicated with me. Boys can't understand that I don't want to kiss them. When they insist, I say I have *philematophobia*. They must think it's some kind of sexually transmitted disease and it puts them off, poor dears. But yesterday, not only did a boy know the word, he even explained it to me: It's because you couldn't get all your words out as a child, he said. I was bowled over. And he's mega cute.

One morning, in the seventh winter, Aunt Anna phoned me. She had received a letter from you. You were on the west coast of Mexico, or so you said. The words didn't say very much, just that perhaps you were not dead. You had a new life and a new friend. I couldn't think of anything else all day. In the evening the shrink thought I looked pale and nervous, which alarmed him. I told him I felt sick. He asked whether I felt sick knowing that you were still alive somewhere. He pressed me on it. No, no, no, I repeated. Then what is it? What is it? I collapsed in tears. All the tears. Niagara Joséphine. I couldn't stop. I got through his box of Kleenex in two minutes flat. He offered me his shirt tail, and that made me laugh through my hiccups. I calmed down a bit. I have others, he added, I have plenty of shirts, and that set me off crying again. Floods of tears. God, I'm useless.

Then he said a lovely thing. I'll never forget it. A birth always involves a lot of water and a lot of tears. Welcome, Joséphine. Welcome.

22/12

The plane leaves in two hours' time. I'm surrounded by people who are off to get some sun. They're deathly pale and they talk non-stop. They're all excited. You'd think silence scared them. I like silence, I like wind, the sound of waves, warmth. Mama shat a brick when I told her I was going, of course she did. She had planned something with the Olive for Christmas, a family thing. You must be joking, I said. So you're not splitting up this Christmas, you're waiting till New Year. Is that it? We're not a family, Mama, only Léon thinks that. But you're not even in his family, his family is the Olive. His biker comrade. *Give me a high five.* One of these days they'll be sharing girls after getting the same tattoo. *Toriwakeru* – to share. He bunks off school and you haven't noticed. He's losing the softness of childhood, your son already looks like a little old man. You haven't looked at anyone but yourself this last year. The little wrinkles close to your eyes, you look at those all the time. The little bulge in your gut. Your jeans half a size bigger, then a whole size. Time is making you crazy. Times passes and things decay. I wanted to talk to you about myself, I wanted to tell you that things can improve with time. But you weren't interested. You didn't see the progress I was making. You didn't see that the slice of ham was fading, the colour was changing to the colour of a turkey escalope and beginning to match my pretty complexion, and that my dimple had come back. You didn't tell me that I was (almost) pretty again. You asked me how I thought you looked, you asked Léon how he thought you looked, it was all about you. I told you that questions like that would make you into one of those women who could be seduced with nothing more than a smile, by the kind of man who'd leave you at dawn. You may be beautiful now but soon you'll just be an easy lay. I always thought you were very beautiful, Mama; when you weren't paying your beauty any attention. When it was a gift. Aunt Anna told me about you and Papa, when you were together. Your passionate early days. My birth. And then your doubts. You already wanted to leave, you weren't sure you'd always love him. Always love us. Did you know that a person can still leave by staying? You're world champion at doing that. I was sad. People grow up twisted without a mother's love, they grow up crooked.

22/12 (later)

I finish my phone call to Sacha. She's at Uriage with her parents, putting up the Christmas tree. She hates all that. I'm hanging my baubles on it, she said. We laughed. I love her laugh. We'll talk again soon.

22/12 (on the plane)

The in-flight entertainment isn't great. The food really isn't great. But at least I don't have a fat woman sitting next to me, or some horrible jerk. I'm next to an old couple. They're holding hands. They aren't talking; I think they're praying. She cut up his chicken breast for him just now, she picked out the peas and the little bits of garlic. He chews slowly. Sometimes she wipes his mouth. She gives him pills every two hours and he struggles to swallow them. She tilts his head back and helps him sip water when he takes the pills. They don't watch any films. They don't read. They don't talk. They just hold hands. Someday I'll hold someone's hand like that, and I'll never be afraid again. Someday. I talked to the shrink a lot about this journey. He thinks I'm ready for it. But I'm still scared. And, at the same time, so happy I've been brave enough to do it. What if . . .? He told me not to ask questions, he said that I'd already chosen the response by going. The journey is more important than the destination. But I think the worst thing would be not to be recognised. To be unknown. That's *desconocido* in Spanish. Then he did an amazing thing. He caressed the left side of my face. He said: That's not going to happen, Joséphine.

I don't know why, but I believed him.

22/12 (on the plane after a siesta)

I've been on the plane for nine hours now and there's still just under four to go. That's a long time. We keep on eating. I watched a James Bond film with Eva Green. She looks like Sacha (or vice versa). There's something in her smile, it's predatory but tender. Super-sexy. The couple beside me are still holding hands. He's gone to sleep with his head on her shoulder. She doesn't dare move in case she wakes him up. Just now I listened to a music channel. It played an old song I didn't know. The words went something like: *Tell me about him / How he's doing now? / Is he happy yet?*[*] It was Niagara Joséphine all over again. Terrible. The lady beside me offered me a handkerchief, moving cautiously because the man was still asleep. And she smiled at me. It was an amazingly human smile.

23/12

I slept for ten hours straight when I reached the hotel. A soft, deep night's sleep. Without dreams. Without shadows. I could do with nights like that all the time. Tomorrow will be my first Christmas on my own. There's music here. Statues of the Virgin Mary. Candles in jars showing the paths taken by souls.

[*] *Parlez-moi de lui* (words Jean-Pierre Lang; music Hubert Giraud, Jean-Pierre Lang, 1973).

In his letter, he told Aunt Anna that he had made a friend here. Pascual. I called the friend at the hotel where they both work. The Desconocido. But you aren't there today. Pascual told me that you were sure to be on the beach at Mayto, in spite of the wind, because the weather is so fine. It's twenty degrees, a perfect December day, a Christmas gift.

He always goes to the part of the beach near the hotel, Pascual continued. It's the only hotel nearby, you can't miss it, Señorita.

I'm on the bus. I'm holding my notebook, the odyssey of my murdered life. My hands are shaking, like Colette's. No doubt because of the bumpy road – it feels like we are driving over corrugated iron. But most of all, I think, because of my fear. No, not my fear. My joy.

I think I must be trembling with joy.

The bus stops to drop me off. The driver points to the far end of the beach. It's windy; the waves are high and stormy. There are no surfers about, the place is practically deserted. I walk slowly. My bare feet sink into the warmth of the sand. A few children are throwing sticks for a dog. I can make out the hotel on the left. It seems to be closed, almost abandoned. A couple are walking beside the foaming water's edge. Sometimes they scurry up the beach to avoid the reach of the waves. I look at them. Particularly at him. No, at you. Now there are three of them, sitting and watching the heavy swell. A man, a woman and a child. Tears immediately come to my eyes. I recognise that neck. That back. That seated figure. He used to look the same when he sat on my bed in the evenings. When he sat cross-legged to read me *Hansel and Gretel*. I'd like to cry out, I'd like to run, but I put my hand to my mouth. My feet won't obey me. They go on walking slowly, they carry me towards the three of them, towards him.

They aren't talking. The child is clutching a football to his chest. The woman's hair whips against my father's face. I am at least five metres away from them. The wind conceals me. Two more steps. The child looks up at the clouds, and then at my father.

Why does it rain, Antonio?

And then I am there with them. I am sitting down

beside my father. He doesn't flinch. He turns his face towards me. He is handsome. He smiles at me. Time has passed. He has placed his hand on my shoulder. His fingers are pressing it gently. He is shedding tears. He will not let me fly away again.

Then he tells the story of Ranginui. He tells the story of Papatuanuku. He tells the tale of the Earth Mother and the Sky Father. He tells the tale of our tears.

Ultimately, then, our lives were worth it all.

Acknowledgements

My thanks again, always and for ever, to Karina Hocine for these six (already) years of Happiness.

To Eva Bredin and the whole brilliant team at Lattès.

Thanks to Kirsty Dunseath and her fabulous team who have helped my books cross the Channel. Thank you to Anthea Bell who has a way of making my words even more beautiful in English.

Thanks to the booksellers who always a find a place to display the books that they like.

Huge, huge thanks to my readers. You are the ones who make the books into good stories. It is you who always have the last word, and it is often rather a nice one.

Thanks to my daughter Grâce, so fitting a name, who allowed me to tame Joséphine. To the writers of the musical *Les Misérables*, after Victor Hugo, who inspired Antoine on p. 111.

And finally, to Dana, who every day gives me the gift of a tomorrow.